Puppy Party

Books by Anna Wilson

The Poodle Problem
The Dotty Dalmatian
The Smug Pug

Puppy Love
Pup Idol
Puppy Power
Puppy Party

Kitten Kaboodle
Kitten Smitten
Kitten Cupid

Monkey Business
Monkey Madness

I'm A Chicken, Get Me Out of Here!

www.annawilson.co.uk

Puppy Party

Anna Wilson

Illustrated by MOIRA MUNRO

MACMILLAN CHILDREN'S BOOKS

First published 2011 by Macmillan Children's Books
a division of Macmillan Publishers Limited
20 New Wharf Road, London N1 9RR
Basingstoke and Oxford
Associated companies throughout the world
www.panmacmillan.com

ISBN 978-0-330-51881-9

3 5 7 9 8 6 4 2

A CIP catalogue record for this book is available from
the British Library.

Printed and bound in the UK by CPI Group (UK) Ltd, Croydon, CR0 4YY

For Malika, with love

Meet the Pups

 Honey

Custard

 Titch

Meatball

1
How to Get Rid of a Bossy Boots Big Sister

When my sister April got married and left home, my first thought was that I would be OVER-THE-TOP-OF-THE-MOON WITH RELIEF AND TOTAL JOY. I mean, what eleven-year-old girl would *not* be happy to finally get rid of a big sister who was DECIDEDLY more ancient than she was, and who was really quite a severely huge Bossy Boots?

I had spent very many of my years on this planet wishing that April would find a place of her own. So when Nick, her boyfriend, asked her to marry him, and then they did *actually really get married* (which was quite a shock for me and

Puppy Party

Mum as, between us, we were not sure that April was mature enough to do such a grown-up thing), I was quite a bit excited about what life would be like Without April. In fact, while she was away on her post-wedding holiday thing, I did a bit of dreaming and Planning For the Future.

Even my pet Labrador, Honey, looked rather perky at the thought of April leaving. Maybe she was thinking that she would no longer have to put up with being called 'that mutt' and other such names of a non-complimentary and OFFENSIVE nature.

'Hey, Honey,' I said to my ever-such-a-gorgeous pooch on April's wedding day (and obviously I said this very quietly so that April did not hear): 'Won't it be great without Bossy Boots Big Sister around? It's just you and me now!'

Who? What? Where?

'Life will be gloriously quiet and a sense of freedom will fill the air every single day of my life from now until the end of eternity,' I said. I was feeling really quite poetical about how utterly marvellous my life would finally be now that I would have some Personal Space. 'It will be like as if I was a butterfly,' I added.

Enough of that — what about a snack?

Mum was extra-specially nice to me around the wedding time, which I at first thought was mightily suspicious. Normally Mum is only extra-specially nice to me if she wants me to do something horrid, like go to the dentist's or eat spinach or have tea with a BORING old person who is a friend of hers but who I don't know or even want to get to know in any way whatsoever. But nothing like that appeared to be on the horizon.

She kept saying things like, 'I know life will seem a bit strange to start with once April's gone, but we'll be all right,' and, 'I will make sure you don't feel lonely, Summer,' and, the most mysterious comment of all, 'Don't *you* go growing up too fast, now, will you?'

As if I, a mere human, have any control over how fast I grow! If people could control how fast they grew, then think of the IMPLICATIONS: in other words, think of what that would mean! Really small people who were fed up with being really small could think extra hard about being tall and make themselves

shoot up a whole metre over night. And really big people could shrink themselves just by Sheer Willpower so that they could fit into the clothes they had always wanted to fit into. And so on and so forth, so that you might actually be able to watch people growing and shrinking all over the place, even on the bus in front of your very eyes! It would be wickedly astounding. Or maybe it wouldn't if it was just Normal Everyday Life . . . Anyway, the fact of the matter was that Mum kept saying cryptical things and being extra-specially nice to me.

I told my Bestest Friend Molly about this.

'Aha!' she said, with a Beady Look in her eye (which does not mean that her eyes had turned into glass ornaments of a jewellery-type nature, but that she looked *sparkly* and alert and full of ideas). 'If your mum is behaving like this, you should take Full Advantage, you know.'

'What?' I asked, puzzled.

5

Puppy Party

'You know what they say: when the cat is away, the mouse will play!' said Molly, wiggling her eyebrows in a mysterious fashion.

When the cat is away, life is pretty dull.

'They may well say that,' I said, 'but the cats are not away: Cheese is sitting on the radiator and

Toast is sitting on Cheese's head. And as far as I know we do not have any mice in this house anyway, so what in all the earth are you talking about in such a riddlesome manner?'

Molly did her immensely exaggerated eye-rolling thing she does when she thinks I am being Dense and Stupid, and said, 'Once April's gone, you'll have to grab your chance to get what you have always wanted!'

The Light Dawned, which is a poetical way of saying that I then in that instant realized what it was that Molly was going on about. I looked at her with my face all beamy and we both said in Unison, 'April's room!'

I had always complained that I had the smallest room in the house. (Well, not as small as the cupboard under the stairs, or the downstairs loo – but obviously those are not proper rooms such as a real person can actually sleep in. I do know this as I once did try to sleep in the cupboard under the stairs when I was exceptionally cross and in a bad frame of mood and wanted to Prove a Point. It was not a comfortable or particularly cosy experience.)

Whenever I tried to Broach the Subject of my

extremely small room, in other words talk about it, all Mum would say was, 'When April leaves home, you can have her room.'

But the trouble was, it had never looked as though April ever *would* leave home. She was certainly old enough to, and she had a job, so it was not as if money was an issue. In my opinion, the problem was that Mum had made it too comfy for April at home: she got all her laundry done and all her meals cooked and she could use Mum's car whenever she wanted and she had even been known to RUN RIOT with Mum's credit card on occasions, so of course April was not in a tearing hurry to leave.

And Mum was equally, most of the time, not in a tearing hurry to *make* her leave, for reasons which frankly escaped me.

Mum would even say things like, 'I do love having my two girls with me. I would miss you so much if you moved out, April.'

How to Get Rid of a Bossy Boots Big Sister

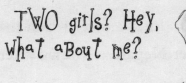 

TWO girls? Hey, what about me?

But then there were times when even Mum could see that April was Taking the Biscuit, which does not mean that she had helped herself to Honey's snacks, but that she was behaving in a rather unacceptable manner. Like the time April had borrowed Mum's special smart jacket out of the wardrobe without asking and had put it back covered in DUBIOUS marks of a strange and unremovable nature.

After that particular incident Mum had said, 'The day you find your own place, April Lydia Love, is a day that cannot come quickly enough for my liking!'

But somehow, both April and I knew deep down that Mum did not mean such things.

And on the day when April did marry Nick,

Puppy Party

Mum blubbed an awful lot, so that proved that she only said the rather Negative Things when April was being a pain.

That was the difference between me and Mum. I most definitely *did* mean the Negative Things that I thought in my head when April was being a pain – and that was most of the time as far as I was concerned.

She was always acting as if I was an irritating little squirt who had to be put up with and was generally in the way and under her feet. And she was such a dramatical drama queen about every single thing in her life, so that Mum and I had to listen to all the Ups and Downs of Life Being April, which frankly wore me out to a frazzle and gave me a headache.

And so I had spent quite a lot of years of time planning what I would do when she finally got Out Of My Hair. (I have actually often wondered about that particular expression, as it

is a bit weird. I
mean, how could
anybody ever
really get stuck
in your hair in
the first place?
They would have
to be extremely
tiny to do it, if you
stop to think about
it. And although
my sister is about as

irritating as the average flea in my own personal
ESTIMATION, she is unfortunately a lot bigger
than even the biggest flea, and causes an awful lot
more trouble.)

In fact, over the years I had even made
a secret list of my reasonings in one of my
notebooks. It went something like this:

WHAT WILL HAPPEN WHEN APRIL'S <u>MOVED OUT</u>!!

1) I will <u>not</u> get bossed about.

2) I will <u>not</u> have to wait five <u>million</u> hours for the bathroom in the morning.

3) I will <u>not</u> have to wait five <u>million</u> hours for the bathroom in the evening.

4) I will <u>not</u> have to listen to her going on about what happened in her <u>boring</u> office.

5) I will <u>not</u> have to lend her my <u>amazing</u> pooch so that she can go on long smoochy walks with her boyfriend.

6) I will <u>finally</u> and eventually get my hands on her <u>ROOM</u>!!

How to Get Rid of a Bossy Boots Big Sister

And I have to say that Reason Number Six was always in actual fact the most important reason of all. So you can see how much I was looking forward to April jolly well going Once And For All.

2
How to Get What You've Always Wanted

During, and indeed after, The Event of the Year, that is to say the wedding, life was pretty hectic. It was also actually stomach-churningly exciting. I should say that in the Normal Run of Things I have never been very interested in marriages and people's love-lives and that sort of general **SMOOCHIFYING** nonsense. But out of the number of possible people in the world for my sister to fall head-over-heels in love with, Nick Harris was quite probably the best. And this was not just because he is a kind and friendly sort of man who does not ever say those super-cringeworthy or boring

How to Get What You've Always Wanted

things like, 'Oh, haven't you grown!' or 'How is school coming along?', but also (and mainly) because he is a vet.

Now you might well ask, 'What exactly is so mind-gogglingly fascinating about being a vet? It is not a mega-cool job like being a celebrity singer or someone on the telly who does those Reality Shows where they put you in a house and watch you turn into a loony.' And you would be right about that last bit. Being a vet is not in the slightest bit like that.

Thank the high heavens above it is *much* more exciting! But then I would say that as I am what some people might call a dog person, which means that I am OVER-THE-TOP-OF-THE-MOON about anything dog-related, and that includes vets. Especially vets like Nick Harris who are extremely knowledgeable and wise when it comes to the subject of the average CANINE, in other words, dog.

It's the Best subject in the World

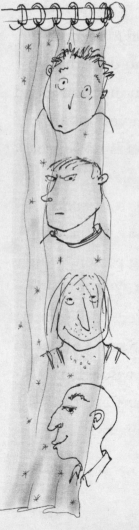

So, as I said, it was really what my best friend Molly Cook would call FORTUITOUS that my sister had had the good sense to marry Nick Harris and not some other useless type of man like the boyfriends she'd had in the past. I will not go into those types. Mum has said it is best that we Draw a Veil over them. I asked Molly what that meant, as she is super-intelligent when it comes to difficult words and expressions. She explained that it did not mean, as I had thought, that we needed to find all of

How to Get What You've Always Wanted

April's old boyfriends and cover them up with some kind of see-throughy fabric, but that 'to draw a veil over' something means that it is best to forget about it.

Back to the wedding.

Even though I was quite insanely happy to think that I would be able to say, 'My brother-in-law is a vet, don't you know?', the most exciting thing about the Big Day was that Honey, my most gorgeous-est pooch, was allowed to be a bridesdog!

It was a special moment.

I know, it's bonkers doolally-crazy, isn't it? But she was! And if you want to see a picture of her and her mum, Meatball (a pooch of extreme adorable-ness who has the misfortune to be owned by sock-stinker extraordinaire, Mr Frank

Gritter himself) then you really should go and get yourself a copy of *Puppy Power* and turn to the back. (Actually what am I *saying*? You shouldn't just turn to the back, you should read the whole thing through from page number one right to the end, obviously!)

Honey and Meatball were the chief bridesdogs, and they had help from two of Honey's own cute pups, Titch (who now belongs to my totally bestest friend in the entire world, Molly Cook) and Cupid (who belongs to Nick and April – yes, they finally got their *own* dog at last).

'Cupid?' I hear you ask. 'Isn't that the most idiotic of names for a golden Labrador?' And you would be right, which is why, thank the high heavens above, Nick managed in the end to gently persuade April that actually it might be better if they called her something else. He did this very cleverly. He waited until April had

had the most **magical** type of wedding she could ever have dreamed of, and he said the most romantic and icky-sloppy stuff about how much he loved her in his speech, and he whirled her around the dance floor as if she was a princess and he was Prince Charming and THEN he very cleverly chose to announce *in public* (well, in front of me and Mum and the people sitting on our table) so that April couldn't go too goggle-eye-mad-as-a-mongoose with anger at him: 'You know, I've been thinking. I don't think Cupid really looks like a Cupid.'

No, I must admit, I don't . . .

'Oh?' said April. Even though she was having the Time of Her Life, she still managed to sound pretty scary and her eyes were STEELY BRIGHT and her lip curled stiffly.

'Mmm,' said Nick, keeping his voice light and airy. 'I think it's because there's this huge beast of a cat who keeps coming into the surgery who's called Cupid. His owner is a teenage girl who's crazy about him and can't see that the name doesn't really suit him. Anyway, it doesn't feel right to me, treating this bruiser of a cat and then coming home and having to call our lovely pup by the same name. Do you think we could call him something else?'

It was pretty obvious from the puzzlement in April's expression that she did not like the idea of a soppy teenage girl calling her cat the same name as their beloved pupsicle. And obviously a Cat Name is not good for a Dog Name. She thought for a moment and said, 'Yes, well. I can see your point.'

And so, thank goodness to gracious, from that day forward Cupid was no longer called by that stupid and frankly outrageously embarrassing name.

How to Get What You've Always Wanted

No, he has a much *more* embarrassing name now.

Custard.

Still, embarrassing name or not, Custard was a gorgeous bundle of poochiness. And I got to know him a whole lot better after the wedding, as he came to stay with us while April and Nick were on honeymoon! It was U**TTER** FAN**TABU-**ℓ**oUSNESS**, as it was like having my own new puppy all over again (except that we knew we would be giving him back in a couple of weeks, so Mum was not even one tiny bit stressed out about it like she had been when Honey was a pup).

Honey loved having Custard around the place, although I did think it sometimes looked as if she was feeling *slightly* like Mum does when the holidays have been going on a bit and Mum starts to say things like, 'Much as I love you, Summer . . . ' and 'The holidays are lovely, but it will be nice to get back to normal,' and 'I do miss a bit of a routine,' and 'Will you PLEASE shut up?'

It's just he's a little, how shall I put it – lively . . .

Custard would jump on top of Honey all the time and barge into her as if she was trying to knock her over, and if Honey had a stick she particularly wanted to have a good chew on, Custard would grab the other end of it and tug and tug. And if Cheese and Toast were being quiet and SNoozY for once, Custard would pounce on them and make them hiss and spit and sometimes scratch Honey if she happened to be in the way.

Honey was quite Understanding and Patient when Custard was being irritating like this and sometimes even seemed to like playing his games with him. But it was always Honey who got tired

first, and that was when Custard would Resort to
Ear-Biting.

**How else do I
get her attention?**

And of course, who in the wide world would like
having their ears bitten? I know I certainly would
not. And Honey did not either. In fact, she made
her feelings Very Clear Indeed. She snapped back.

It's the only language
these youngsters understand.

I was shocked the first time that it happened. I
had never seen Honey bite anything that was
not food or a special dog toy. She had never
bitten me or Molly or even Frank Gritter (who is
possibly the only human I would actually myself
consider biting, he is sooo annoying sometimes).

Puppy Party

When this ear-biting started, Mum began to get a bit FRAZZ*L*ED with having Custard around the place too.

'It's not that I don't love him,' said Mum one morning. (Here we go, I thought.) 'But I do feel sorry for poor Honey, and this house is not really big enough for two dogs to be constantly careering around the place. I have to say I will be glad when April and Nick are back.'

I could see what Mum meant, but I was not that keen on the idea of Custard leaving us. And at the time I wasn't that thrilled about April coming back either as I thought she would walk right back in and be her usual Bossy Boots self and go on and on about how amazing her honeymoon had been.

However, when I complained about these things to Molly, she did point out the one majorly good thing about April coming back from honeymoon.

How to Get What You've Always Wanted

'Now's your chance, Summer,' she said in a Conspiratorial Moment the day before April got back. 'The bedroom is all yours!'

And though I am now ashamed to say it, I beamed and stuck both my thumbs up in a **Gesture of Glee.**

3
How to Entirely
Decluttervate

However, I *didn't* get to move into April's room the day she got back from honeymoon. I was quite cross about this, but Mum said, 'I'm afraid there is no way you can until April has cleared out all her stuff.'

Now April had promised to do this straight away after coming back, but as with a lot of my sister's promises, they never get carried out exactly To The Letter. In other words, April is very good at saying one thing and doing another.

For a start, when she and Nick came back, they wanted to redecorate Nick's flat, 'And to make the job easier, we need to keep the rooms clear of stuff,' April explained. 'I cannot possibly take boxes of stuff back to the flat and leave them lying around while we decorate. It is bad enough having a puppy about the place.'

Who's bad?

What April did not explain, was that it would take her and Nick weeks and utterly *weeks* to do their redecorating. But at last and after an entire EᗡERNIᘔY, the day came when April took the last box of her stuff away from the house and her room was empty.

The minute she had left the building, I was on the phone to Molly.

'She's done it! She's gone!' I squealed. 'The room is mine, all mine!' I cackled in a **fiendishly evil master-criminal** type of a way.

Puppy Party

'I'm coming round right this minute!' Molly squealed back.

And she did.

'Do you know what kind of a Look you want to go for?' was her first question.

We were standing in April's room, which was by now completely empty apart from her bed and a chest of drawers and Cheese, who had taken to hiding in there from Toast and Honey (except there wasn't anywhere really for him to hide, so he was just a cat in a room).

 Hey, I've found my own space. Don't knock it.

The room looked even more vaster now that it had no clothes and make-up and hairdryers and magazines CLUttERED all about the place.

Honey was sitting at my feet inspecting the empty room and peering at Cheese as though she'd never set eyes on him before. Cheese arched his back and hissed, but gave up when it was clear Honey was not going to do anything. I looked at my pooch quizzically and wondered what was going through her mind.

Never Been in here Before in my life. That puppy looks vaguely familiar though . . .

'Summer?' Molly said, snapping me back from my wonderings.

'Oh, erm. I had not really thought of a Look exactly,' I admitted. 'I had only ever dreamed of how utterly fantastical it would be to have all this space just for me. And how it would be BRILLIANTISSIMO for you to be able to come for a sleepover without me having to clear a patch on the floor among my heaps of stuff.'

'Mmm,' said Molly, raising one eyebrow.

'That would be good, yes.'

I looked at the walls which were a bit dirty and sad-looking now that all April's pictures and posters had gone. 'I think more than anything we need to just get on and paint the walls,' I said, in as decisive a tone as I could manage.

'And what colour were you thinking of?' Molly asked.

'I, er . . . green?'

Molly raised her eyes to the heavens. 'You need to be rather more clearer than that!' she said impatiently. 'Look, I have brought some magazines to give us Inspiration.' And she fished around inside her bag and pulled out a bundle of shiny glossy magazines with names such as *Spectacular Skirting Boards* and *Wonderful Wallpapers*.

Who in the name of sanity comes up with whole magazines about such yawnsome things? I thought.

I was about to say so, but Molly had already flicked open *Wonderful Wallpapers* and was gushing in an over-the-top manner about something called a 'feature wall', which apparently is when you only put wallpaper on one wall and you paint the remaining three walls. I thought that would look bizarre and freaky, as though you only had enough money to decorate one wall and then had to stop. But I did not have a chance to squeeze a word in edgeways, or front ways or any old way, because Molly was chattering on almost without breathing.

'And it really is the best and most fashionable thing for Interior Design these days,' she was saying. 'I saw it all on this faberoony programme about moving house and redecorating and so on.'

I should have known really that the only reason that Molly was excited about me moving into April's room was so that she could come round and Take Over in that way she has. She was clearly obsessed with this Interior Design thing. Why on earth it is called that, I don't know. It is just a posh way of saying 'decorating'. There is not much that is Design about it if you ask me. You just say, 'That wall should be purple,' and 'The bed cover should have stars on it,' and then you go to a shop which sells those things and you get them and hey presto! The room is decorated. The Interior bit is a load of utter randomness too, as how can you decorate the Interior of a wall? It is the EXTERIOR, in other words the outside, of a wall that you put the paint on. You do not peel off the surface of the wall and stick your hands into the bricky stuff and do the painting there.

How to Entirely Decluttervate

'We must make a List of all the things we need to progress the designing of the Interior of your new room,' Molly was saying bossily. 'And I have to tell you, Summer, that we should crack on with the designing and updating of your new room BEFORE you start moving your stuff in. On the extremely informative TV programme *Moving On Up*, the presenter and designer Farrah Ball is always saying that you must start with a Clean Slate, in other words you must clear out and Declutter all your junk before you redecorate.'

'Excuse *me*!' I said, feeling rather quite a bit outraged. 'I have not got a lot of *junk* that needs *decluttervating*, thank you very much.'

Molly took me by the hand and led me into my room. We stood in the doorway, which to be honest was the only place we could stand as the floor was a bit covered in clothes and stuff. Honey bounded across a jumpery-type mound and plonked herself down on my duvet which had somehow found itself trailing over the side of my bed.

'It's that Lived-In Look,' I muttered.

In other words, 'messy', which is just the way we like it.

Molly put her hands on her hips while she cast a glance around my room. Her top lip curled and her nose wrinkled in an expression of what could only be described as utter DISTASTE. In other words, she looked as if my stuff was giving off a **bad smell**.

'Mmm,' she said. 'That is one way of putting it.'

'What do you mean?' I said.

'Never mind,' said Molly. She was now in Brisk and Efficient mode. 'I have got a truly

How to Entirely Decluttervate

Masterly Plan as to how we can get your room made-over and gorgeous in a super-fast time.'

I sighed noisily. When Molly is on a roll like this, there is no stopping her (unless you want to have a major falling out, which is never pleasant and not to be recommended). 'So tell me,' I said.

Molly beamed and whipped out one of her notebooks. Now, I like notebooks (who doesn't?)

but Molly really is the *Queen of Notebooks*, not to mention the *Most Majestical-on-High of Lists*.

She began by wittering on again about the TV programme, which apparently gave all sorts of tips and hints about decluttervating. 'First of all you need coloured stickers so that you can go round your room and divide your possessions and books and things into piles that say "Keep", "Throw Out" and "Maybe". Luckily I have come prepared.'

She flipped open the cover of her notebook and there were three sheets of coloured stickers: one sheet of pink, one of blue and one of yellow. 'We can use the pink for "Keep", the blue for "Throw Out" and the yellow for "Maybe".'

It looked as though I was not going to have a say in a single thing. I wondered if I was going to be allowed to say exactly WHAT I wanted to 'Keep', etc. Possibly not at the rate Molly was going.

How to Entirely Decluttervate

Just as long as I'm in the 'Keep' pile.

Molly busied herself around my old room. She walked up and down, scribbling things in her notebook and eyeing objects in the way people do on those programmes like *Money for Old Rope* where they look at the stuff you've been keeping in your attic and try and guess if it is worth anything at all. (Often it is not.) She picked up a lamp, sighed a bit, then put it down. Then she picked up my favouritest pair of huge **BOBBLY** ladybird slippers that make my feet look as massive as a clown's and which are the most cosiest footwear ever to be invented. She was holding them sort of between one finger and thumb as if they stank as badly as Frank Gritter's socks.

This is when I got rather angry. 'What are you going to tell me is wrong with my ladybird slippers?' I shouted.

I happen to think they're rather tasty.

Molly dropped them in shock. 'Oh, er, nothing at all!' she protested, hastily grabbing a pink sticker and slapping it on to the slippers. 'They are *definitely* going into the "Keep" pile.'

I walked over and held out my hand. 'I will have those pink stickers, please,' I said. Molly could see that I Meant Business, which does not mean that I was about to open a shop and try to sell the contents of my old room. It means that I was mega-serious about being in control of this particular plan.

And so we spent a whole day dividing my stuff into piles. And actually, though I do hate to admit it when Molly is right, I have to say that it was quite a THERAPEUTIC exercise, which is a posh word for saying that I quite enjoyed myself. Honey gave up on anything interesting happening and settled down for a snooze.

Mum came in at one point with some biscuits and some orange squash. She nearly tripped over the "Maybe" pile when she opened the door, and the glasses of squash TEETERED slightly on the tray.

'Oh my goodness, Summer!' she gasped, as she struggled to rescue the drinks. 'What on earth are you two up to?'

Molly explained her Masterly Plan, making sure Mum knew that it had been all her idea.

Mum literally beamed from one ear right across to the other. 'What a marvellous idea, Molly!' she said. 'I think we'll have to enlist you to go through the rest of the house. I have been trying to get my daughters to sort out their stuff for years. Oh . . .' Her beaminess was very suddenly switched to a MELANCHOLY sort of

mood, in other words she suddenly looked sad.
'What I meant to say is, now that April's gone,
it's a good chance for you and me to organize
ourselves, Summer, isn't it? Just the two of us, I
mean.' She hastily put down the tray of drinks
and biscuits on my old music box which was in
the 'Throw Out' pile (because it played a 'babyish
and somewhat annoying tune' according to
Molly) and left us to it.

Molly narrowed her eyes and chewed in the
corners of her mouth as Mum shut the door.
'Mmm,' she said.

'What?' I asked, picking up a glass of squash
and taking a SWIG (which is a piratical word for
gulping down a drink in a thirsty fashion).

'I think your Mum is suffering from Empty
Nest Syndrome,' said Molly, still narrowing her
eyes in a thoughtful manner.

'What in the highest heavens are you
wittering on about now, Molly?' I asked. 'Mum is

not a bird-watching type of person and probably
wouldn't even notice if there was a FULL nest in
our garden, let alone an empty one—'

'No, no!' Molly laughed in a grown-up way.
'It doesn't have anything to do with nests!'

'But you just said—'

'"Empty Nest Syndrome" is an expression,'
said Molly, in an over-the-top patient manner. 'It
is what you say about a mother when her children
have left home. It means that the mother gets
sad. Apparently birds and other animals in nature
behave in a bizarre way when their young have
left – or Flown the Nest.'

I felt kinda down
when my pupsicles
left home . . .

'But I haven't left or Flown the Nest,' I said,
puzzled. 'I am only sorting out my bedroom so

that I can move into April's.'

'Exactly,' said Molly pointfully. 'April has moved out of your family's "nest", so leaving it a – bit – emp-ty – get it?' she added, slowing her voice right down to the level people use to talk to immensely stupid other people.

I would have got offended under normal circumstances at being talked to like this, but the words Molly had said caused a sudden and vast BRAINFLASH to occur to me, and I all at once realized what it was that Molly was saying: Mum was sad because April had moved out (although why she could not have said that in plain and decent English instead of going on about nests, I don't know).

In an instant a wave of sadness and sympathetic feeling washed over me and I wanted to rush out and give Mum a ginormous hug and tell her it was OK because she still had me and Honey.

How to Entirely Decluttervate

'Wh-what do you think I can do to make Mum feel better?' I asked, flumping down on to my favouritest beanbag, which had a pink 'Keep' sticker on it.

Molly was tapping her teeth with her pencil, which is what she quite often does when she is deep in thought.

'I think your mum needs a large dose of distractivation,' she said finally. 'In other words, we have to come up with something to keep her occupied so that she doesn't think about April not being here. I feel the need for another dose of Masterly Planning.'

I agreed, but secretly hoped whatever Molly came up with wouldn't involve a Total and Complete Decluttervating of the Entire Contents of our house.

4

How to Realize You Miss Something Once It's Gone

It was getting close to the Easter holidays by now, and I had only just been able to at last move into my new room. It had certainly been a huge PALAVER, but it had been good as it had been distractivating for Mum as well as me (mainly because she spent a lot of time and energy going to the paint shop for me to change paints when I didn't like them). Cheese and Toast had been very unimpressed by the whole upheaval and had gone into major sulk mode (which is not that different from their usual mode of being, if I'm totally honest). Life had been full and busy and totally hectic.

How to Realize You Miss Something Once It's Gone

However, now the holidays were nearly
upon us (which does not mean they were about
to come crashing down around our ears, but
that it was nearly Easter time) I was beginning
to worry that without all the distractivating and
decluttervating, Mum might go back to thinking
about her nest being empty.

I wondered if I should talk to Molly about
this one day after school while we were walking
our pooches together in the park.

I should break off from the NARRATIVE (in
other words story) at this point to explain that
there was a time when it would have been
impossible to even *think* of saying that last
sentence. Molly's mum had always very definitely
been what you might call Not That Keen on
Dogs, and would say things like, 'If you think
you're getting a puppy just because your best
friend has one, you have got another think

coming, Miss Molly.' I used to wonder how on earth Mrs Cook would know that Molly had Other Thinks Coming. Was she perhaps one of those types of people who could read your very mind? But I soon realized that this was not what Mrs Cook meant. What she meant was what my mum says whenever I ask her if Honey can have another litter: 'Over My Dead Body!' In other words, NO.

Don't remind me!

So Molly was not the only one to be totally flabbergasted and bewildified when her mum came and saw Honey's puppies, took one look at Titch (who obviously was the smallest – with a name like that it is not really **Rocket Science**) and went all melty and gooey and speechless for words.

How to Realize You Miss Something Once It's Gone

I have that effect on people. "

Titch had settled into the Cook family right away (well, once he had learned all the Dos and Don'ts about where he could sit and couldn't sit and where he was allowed to breathe in public . . .) and Molly was actually doing quite a good job of training him. So we had got to the stage where we could go for a walk in the park without anything too disastrous happening.

And so that is what we were doing that afternoon, to get back to the story, I mean NARRATIVE . . .

I had been thinking about puppies and the fun we had used to have when April was there and the fact that the puppies had all gone to new homes, rather like April had, and I had just got to the point of sadly wondering if the puppies missed

each other at all, when I heard Molly's voice go
Up a Notch and sound a bit alarmingly nagging in
tone. I quickly tuned back in.

'What is the matter with you, *Summer*?' she
snapped. 'You have not been listening to one
single word that I have been saying to you.'

'Er – sorry?' I said, shaking my head blearily
and coming out of my weirdly sad mood.

Molly tutted noisily. 'Honestly, Summer
Holly Love, you are being extremely strange
these days. If I did not know you better I would
say that you are actually being quite Depressive
about something. But I know that cannot be true
as you are not a Depressive sort of a person. So
I can only think that you are just not listening to
me because you have got something else more
important to think about, in which case perhaps I
should just go home on my own and—'

'Actually,' I broke into Molly's TIRADE of
nonsense rambling and said in a quiet but firm

voice. 'I have realized that I *am* quite a little bit Depressive some of the time these days.'

Molly's expression on her face changed from outraged to perplexed in one split of a moment. 'Oh?' was all she could manage in response.

'Yes,' I said, blinking a bit, as my eyes were feeling hot and prickly. 'I am a bit sad.'

Molly at once flung an arm around me and said, 'But this is terrible! You must tell me all about it at once and right this minute.' And she pushed me down on to a park bench that luckily happened to be close by, otherwise I might have ended up falling on my bottom.

We let the dogs off the lead and sat watching them romp around.

He may Be a titch, But he keeps me on my paws!

49

Then Molly coughed loudly and said, 'So?'

I took a very deep breath, so deep that I managed to inhale a passing fly, which was not a good start, as I had to get over a bit of a choking and spitting fit, but it did at least mean that I did not actually cry. At last I squeaked: 'It's just that I didn't realize I would feel this way, and I almost think it's a bit silly of me, but – I miss April.'

Molly gasped. Her mouth was hanging open so wide I said, 'You'll swallow a fly too if you're not careful.'

She snapped her jaws firmly shut and crossed her arms tightly in front of her chest and then said, through teeth that were clamped together against MARAUDING insects: 'I cannot *believe* you, Summer!'

I frowned and blushed a bit. 'Why not?'

Molly rolled her eyes as impressively as I have ever seen her do, and flinging her arms up in the air, she cried: 'One minute you are saying you

can't wait for your, and I quote, "Bossy Boots Big
Sister" to leave home and you are doing all that
work moving into her room – and saying how
you love having the TV and the sofa and your
mum to yourself in the evenings – and the next
minute you are turning into a Depressive Person
and WEE*p*ING AND WAI*l*ING about it.'

'I am *not* weeping and wailing!' I said in a
protesting sort of way. 'And anyway, you have
never had a Bossy Boots Big Sister to get annoyed
with, or indeed miss, so how in all the earth
would you know how I am feeling?'

Molly sighed and glanced at me in a rather
CONDESCENDING fashion. Then she spoke
in the sort of voice grown-ups use when they are
talking to very small children or animals. 'I am
sorry that you feel so sad, Summer. What can we
do to help?'

What can WE do to help? What in the
highest of all heavens above was she babbling on

about? Had she actually become *two* people or
did she have an
imaginary friend
sitting next to
her? Or did she
suddenly think
she was the Queen
(who was the only
person I had ever
heard of who referred
to herself as 'we' in that
especially *royal* manner
of speaking)?

I was getting really quite
moody now. I ignored Molly and stood up and
called for Honey to come. She is such a good
and obedient poochical these days that she came
immediately right away. I wish I could say the
same for Titch.

How to Realize You Miss Something Once It's Gone

Hey! What are you saying?

He must have found something truly honksome
to roll about in, because as Honey came bounding
towards me, I saw him flip over on to his back
and have a good old rub and ROLLICK on
the grass. He had his eyes closed and his tongue
was lolling out of one side of his mouth and
he was wagging his tail madly — which is quite
impressively difficult, I would imagine, when you
are lying on your back and rolling around, but
somehow he was managing to do it.

I'll do anything
for a honksome whiff!

The result was that something pooey and brown
was being flicked all around the place and Titch's
beautiful golden coat was getting well and truly

trashed. Molly had not noticed, as she was too busy looking at me in a sorrowful way and talking in a PATRONIZING and annoying tone.

'Well,' I said as carelessly as I could manage, 'It's very lovely of you to be Concerned About my Welfare, Molly, but I have to go now as I have rather a lot more homework to do this evening. I will see you tomorrow. Come on, Honey.'

Just when it was getting interesting . . .

When I got home, Mum was sitting at the kitchen table with her head propped up by her hands as if it would fall off unless she held it there. Her face was looking what can only be described as Glum and her cup of tea had gone cold and the surface of it had that kind of yucksome grimbleshanks **SLIMY SKIN** on it which happens when the milk has gone all floaty.

How to Realize You Miss Something Once It's Gone

'Hi, Mum!' I said, trying to sound cheery. My voice did a funny echoey sound around the walls. Oh my goodness dearie me, the house sounded as empty as I felt.

'What?' said Mum. 'Oh hello, darling. It's you.'

Yes, it is me. You do have another daughter who still lives at home and who is called Summer, and that is actually me.

'How was your day?' Mum asked. But it didn't sound as though she was particularly interested. I could have said, 'Great, thanks, Mum. The teacher made us eat slugs for lunch and run ten miles in the pouring rain in PE,' and she would not have taken any notice. She had not *even* noticed that Honey had trodden muddy paw prints all over the clean kitchen floor tiles.

Just doing my own 'spots' of Interior Designing. (Tee hee!)

Puppy Party

I decided to concentrate on sounding extremely chirpy in the hope it would wake Mum up a bit.

'Oh, my day was super-duper OVER-THE-TOP marvellous!' I said. My voice ended in a funny squeak, which made Mum peer at me strangely. I carried on babbling, 'Yes, I had a lovely, *lovely* day at school and then I took Honey to the park just now with Molly and Titch, and the pooches ran around and were EXCEEDINGLY happy and Molly and I had a jolly good Chin-Wag.'

I paused. And then, totally unexplainably and completely out of nowhere, my bottom lip started to wobble and I plonked myself down in the chair opposite Mum and my shoulders sagged and my head fell on to my chest and my eyes went hot.

'Oh, darling!' Mum cried, suddenly all DISTRAUGHT. 'What on earth is the matter? You haven't had another falling out with Molly, have you? It's not that Rosie Chubb again, is it? I—'

How to Realize You Miss Something Once It's Gone

'NO!' I shouted. Why do mums always do this? They ask you a question and then they go and try and answer the question themselves before you have had a chance to draw one single breath and speak out loud yourself.

Mum stopped in mid–speech and looked rather a little bit horrified. But at least she did not start talking again.

I sighed very deeply and then said, 'I am feeling sad. But if I tell you why, I think you might just laugh at me.'

Mum frowned and shook her head ever so slightly. Then she said in a very softly spoken voice, 'No, Summer. I don't think I will.'

'OK,' I said. Then I paused for dramatical effect (and also to check that Mum really was *not* going to laugh). 'I didn't think this would happen, in fact, I was sure I would feel totally utterly the opposite way about it, but as it has turned out . . . I miss April!' My voice did the squeaky thing again, and I started sobbing like a loop-the-loop loony. Honey whined and left the room.

I don't like that noise. I'm outta here.

Mum pushed her chair back gently and came round to my side of the table and put her arms around me and gave me the sort of calming cuddle that only mums know how to give.

Then she kissed the top of my head and said quietly, 'I know, I know,' and waited until my blubbing had settled down a bit. Then she let go of me and drew up a chair next to me and held my hands.

I sniffed and hiccuped and said, 'It's completely weird. I was absolutely desperate for April to go and get married and let me have her room and not be here to boss me around all the time, but now that I have finally got what I wanted, nothing feels right.'

Mum nodded. She looked a bit blurry through all the tears that were still spilling over the edge of my eyelids.

'And I thought it would be so cool to have the sofa to myself and to be able to watch all the telly programmes I wanted to instead of having to creep around the place while April and Nick snogged on the sofa.' I shuddered a slightly tiny bit when I said that. Even on their wedding day, which is a day when as everyone knows, the couple are allowed to snog in public, it is not something I wanted to have to witness. 'But actually I think I would prefer April to be here snogging Nick,' I continued, 'or even having a tantrum about me using her hairbrush or *something*, because at least then she would STILL BE HERE.'

I stopped to take a breath and try to stop all the hiccupy sobbing. 'It is funny, isn't it?'

murmured Mum. 'The house just feels too quiet.'
Then she went quiet herself and stared into the
distance in a PENSIVE manner.

I was about to go and switch on the telly and
try and convince myself that sitting on the sofa on
my own was as good as I had hoped it would be,
when Mum suddenly said, 'I know – let's have a
party!'

Now, I can assure you that I like a party
as much as anyone in the entire universe likes
a party (which is a lot, unless you are the sort
of person in the entire universe who does *not*,
in which case you are frankly a bit odd in my
opinion), but even I did think that this was
strange timing.

'That is a freaky announcement to make
when we are both feeling so Glum and Down in
the Dumps,' I said.

Mum beamed and jumped up and gave me a
hug and said, 'I know!' in a bit of a loony high-

pitched tone of speaking. And then she said, 'But we could have a party for *April*!'

Then I felt all BEAMY AND LOONY as well, and I squeezed Mum hard and said, 'Yay!'

Mum pulled me back to the kitchen table and made me sit down and then she started talking in a mega-hyper way. 'It's her birthday in, what, two weeks?' she wibbled, counting the days on her fingers. (Why is it OK for grown-ups to do this, but when children do they are told off for cheating and not using their times tables and Mental Maths?) 'And it's quite a special one as it's the first birthday she is going to have as a married woman, and I don't think she and Nick have got enough room in their flat to have a party, so we can just have it here! And we can do it as a SURPRISE!'

I did actually squeal rather loudly when she said this last bit, as I was finding all her excitement quite a bit infectious and I do love a SURPRISE myself.

Puppy Party

'Yippeeee!' I said. I leaped out of my chair and did a bit of a victory dance around the table, punching my fist in the air and chanting, 'We're going to have a PAR-*TEE*! It's going to be a SUR-*PRISE*!'

Mum laughed and Honey came crashing back and joined in all the hoo-ha with a good session of barking and tail wagging.

No idea What's going on, But I'm up for it!

5
How to Come Up with a Theme

Mum suggested that we get on with doing some planning right that instant.

'We should start with a guest list,' she said, getting up and RUMMAGING around in the drawer which is supposed to have useful things like pens and paper in, but which actually has things like old rolls of finished Sellotape, broken hair grips and weird crumb stuff of a dubious and questionable nature (which could be pencil shavings or could be something much worse, so it's best not to Go There).

I'll go there for you if you like!

'OK,' I said. 'Well I suppose we should invite
Nick and some of Nick's friends from the vet's
and – oh no! She might actually want to have
Mr Stingy and Mr Gross from the lawyery
place where she works! And there will be those
annoying friends of hers from college and—'

'Summer! Summer!' Mum was waving her
hands in front of my face to get my attention in
the sort of way people do when someone is Away
With the Fairies, in other words On Another
Planet, in *other* other words, not concentrating on
what is actually going on in the real live world.

'Ye-es?' I said, stopping my Ranting and
Raving for a moment.

'I think that the whole point of a surprise
party is that April is *not* the one organizing
it,' Mum said carefully, looking at me in a
Meaningful way with her eyebrows lowered and
her eyes glinting. She waited for her words to
sink in.

How to Come Up with a Theme

'Aha!' I said, pointing my finger in the air like a scientist who has just discovered the cure for all illness and evil in the world. 'You mean, we can invite whoever *we* want? Oh well, in that case I'm going to ask Molly and Frank and—'

Don't forget the pooches . . .

'Stop! Stop!' Mum cried, laughing and trying to look serious at the same moment. 'I didn't mean that: I meant that April will not be in charge, as it's going to be a surprise. But that doesn't mean you can go ahead and invite only *your* friends: it's still *April's* birthday, don't forget!'

I felt all the fizzle go away for the second time that morning and slumped back into my chair. Much as I missed April, I did not think that I wanted to have a houseful of her boring grown-up friends around the place, balancing a paper plate and a glass and nibbling on one crisp at a time and saying things like, 'I absolutely think this country is going to the dogs,' and other stupid phrases. (People actually do say that, you know, and I have never understood it, as the dogs are very obviously not in control of this country whatsoever. If they were, then it would be *them* taking *us* out for walks and throwing sticks for us to fetch and we would be forced to eat smelly dog food out of tins while they ate roast beef and sausages.)

Sounds good to me.
When does this happen?

How to Come Up with a Theme

I did a big 'humpfing' sound to show my complete disapproval of the whole idea and sank down into my chair as far as I could in a very impressively **SULKY** type of attitude.

'Summer,' said Mum, 'if you will just give me one second to explain the idea I've had?'

'Humpf,' I said again.

Mum sighed loudly and said, 'What about if you and Molly were allowed to do absolutely all the organizing and choose all the food, the decorations and everything with no help from me? And you can ask another of your friends along too, if you want?'

Now this was what is called An Offer You Cannot Refuse.

'Yeeeehah!' I yelled, leaping up out of my chair for the second time during this conversation and dancing an even madder and

loop-the-loop-the-loop dance than the one I had danced before. 'Hooray and yippi-di-do-dah!' I added For Good Measure.

What aBout my friends?

I had to get on the phone at once and immediately to Molly, of course. There is nothing she likes better than a party. And if it is a surprise party then that is, as she would say, 'So Much The Better' (which I have always thought is a bit of a weirdo and slightly Shakespearical way of speaking, but Molly thinks it is more sophisticateder than just speaking the Plain Queen's English).

'Molleeeeee!' I said, when she answered the phone, which is the way I always say her name when I have something exciting-making to say to her. It's kind of our special code, to prepare her for what might come next, in other words an announcement of a highly fanterabulous nature.

How to Come Up with a Theme

'I'm sorry, who is this?' said Molly, in an I'm-
being-a-snotty-grown-up tone of talking.

'Er, it's me!' I said.

'And who is "me"?' she went on in the same
huffy way.

And then I remembered that I had kind
of run off when we had been in the park and
I realized Molly was Making A Point of being
annoyed with me, so I said, 'Molls, I am sorry
I was grumpy, but I have got some ultra-mega-
tastical news to tell you, so please can you forgive
me and just listen a minute?'

'O - k a a a a y,' Molly said, dragging the
word out as if it was a vastly heavy object of an
immovable nature. I decided to
ignore this and Ploughed On
Regardless (which does not
mean that I decided to do a
spot of farming, but that I
carried on talking).

Puppy Party

'Mum has said I can organize a surprise party for April in two weeks' time on her birthday which is April 13th and I can ask you to help me and actually come to the party too and I can have another friend as well if I want, which I think I do want as then it would not be just a boring grown-ups' party where they talk about the weather and the government and tell us how tall we are all getting, and—'

'Whooppppeeeee!' shouted Molly, which was good as it gave me a chance to actually breathe and stop myself from going purple in the face and possibly faint. It also gave me a chance to feel **flooded** with a sense of relief that she was no longer cross with me. 'I am coming round right now,' she said excitedly. 'Do not move or do ANYTHING without me.'

I hesitated for a milli-second and then said, 'Erm – can I put the phone down?'

CLICK.

How to Come Up with a Theme

That was Molly putting the phone down at her house. 'OK,' I thought. 'It's probably all right for me to do that too: putting the phone down could not possibly count as actually moving, could it?' Then I thought, 'How will I go to open the door if I am not allowed to "move or do anything"?'

'MUM!' I shouted. 'Molly is coming round in about a few minutes and she has said I must not move, so will you answer the door?'

Mum came out into the hall and looked at me weirdly and said, 'What on earth are you talking about, Summer?'

Just then the doorbell went, so I gestured to the door with a flick of my head, and Mum sighed and went to open it.

'Hello, Molly,' said Mum. 'Do come in. Apparently I have just been employed as Summer's own personal slave.'

Molly curled her lip in puzzlement and said, 'What?'

Mum shook her head, 'Nothing. Come in.'

Molly ran up to me and squealed. 'I've brought one of my new notebooks especially so that we can start planning and Making Lists! Let's go!'

'You told me not to move,' I said.

'You can be one hundred and ten per cent der-brainish, sometimes,' she said, but in a sort of friendly way, with her head on one side. 'I meant it FIGURATIVELY, not Absolutely Literally,' she explained.

'Oh RIGHT!' I laughed in response to Molly. 'Come on then!' And we did literally zoom up to my room with Honey hot on our heels. Once she was in safely, I slammed the door behind us and we started planning.

Now, as I have already mentioned Molly is RENOWNED in our school for being the Queen of Notebooks, but this new one which she had brought with her was

something else. In fact, I would say that it should have been protected by a law for the Protection of Areas of Stationery of *Outstanding Beauty*. It had a cloth sort of cover like an Olden Fashioned Days reading book and it had gold sticky-uppy letters on it. And it also had a swirly purple and light blue pattern all over it like a kaleidoscope pattern when you look down the tube and turn the bottom bit. It made me SOLWH (which is a short-for type of language that Molly and I have invented for: 'Sigh Out Loud With Happiness').

Molly did a beamy smile of satisfaction. 'It is mega-lush, isn't it? I am only going to write in my most neatest handwriting in it, and I am only going to use these really thin propellery pencils on the pages so that if I make a HIDEOUS mistake, I can rub it out and it will not have spoilt the general beauty of the thing,' she said importantly.

I did agree that it was important not to spoil it.

'Now first of all we must decide on a THEME,' said Molly.

I would say a pooch-styled theme would be a good one.

'Mmm,' I said. 'But I am not one hundred and ten per cent certain that April will like having a party with a theme.'

'Oh, she'll like it all right,' said Molly. 'People always do. My auntie had a party for her fiftieth or something – it was one of those big parties people have for an Old Age. It might have been forty or even sixty, actually . . . Anyway, who cares? She just got old. The important thing is that she had a theme which was basically "silver", so the house was decorated in silver things and everyone came wearing something silver and it was MEGA as I was allowed to buy some shoes that were actually silver! So what

How to Come Up with a Theme

I say is, if you can have a theme when you have got to one of those ancient ages, then why not have one when you are young like April?'

'April is not YOUNG!' I exclaimed. 'And I do not want to wear silver shoes, thank you very much. They will not go with my auburn shade of hair.'

'I am not suggesting we copy the exact theme that my auntie had, for heaven's above sake,' said Molly impatiently. 'And April may not be young, but she does still like to go out and have fun at least, so we should make sure that this party of hers is the most fun ever.'

'Mmm,' I said again.

'So,' said Molly, after she had sat and tapped her pencil against her teeth for a while and I had started daydreaming and yawning. 'How can we make this party totally different and special?'

We both went silent. Honey got bored and

padded over from where she had been sniffing around by my bed and put her head in my lap and sighed very loudly.

I'll say it again – POOCH PARTY!

I stroked Honey's head as I thought and I looked into her chocolatey brown eyes . . . And that is when I had my most SPECTACULAR wave of brain activity that I have ever had (almost).

'PUPPIES!' I shouted, punching the air in a triumphalist salute.

Finally!

I grinned at my Best Friend, expecting that she would join in with my victorious feelings, but she was looking at me with an expression which said, 'You are the looniest loony tune on Radio Loony and I am going to switch you off in a minute.'

'What?' I said, my grin fading fast.

'Er – "What?" yourself,' said Molly.

'Eh?' I said. This conversation was going to turn into a very boring one unless we were careful.

'"Puppies" *what*?? Why do you always have to bring puppies into everything? I mean, I love puppies of course I do, but puppies and parties do not mix, not unless the party is FOR the puppy, which in this case it is most definitely not. Not unless there is a particular puppy who is having a birthday any time soon – oh!'

And finally she did at last stop talking and had a bit of a Light-Bulb Moment herself and she realized what it was that was making me so excited and victoriously triumphalist.

'Honey's birthday!' I said, nodding, as the face of my Best Friend lit up and looked how mine felt – tight and smiley and sparkly with happiness at my Very Brilliant Idea.

I was trying to
tell you . . .

'Honey's birthday is the same week as April's as
it so happens – remember Frank told us she was
born at Easter that time he came into school and
announced that "A Dog is for Life, not Just for
Christmas" and we all teased him because it had
just been Easter?'

'YES!' said Molly and she began scribbling
furiously in her Notebook of Outstanding
Beauty in a way that was not at all mindful of its
specialness, in other words she was not using her
bestest writing but rather making a bit of a big old
scribble in it.

This is what she wrote:

How to Come Up with a Theme

APRIL'S/HONEY'S SURPRISE
BIRTHDAY PARTY

April- Guests
Me
Summer
Summer's mum
Nick
all the other usual boring
grown-up friends

Honey- Guests

Titch (obviously)
April's dog (even more obviously)
Meatball? (nice dog, shame about
the owner, i.e. Frank Gritter)

pong!

[I should point out that this last bit was Molly's opinion. Frank can be quite a laugh.]

'We need to think about food too,' I pointed out. 'And decorations and stuff. Mum has said we can have a Budget.'

'Faberoony!' Molly cried. 'So let's brainstorm food, then.' And she scribbled away some more.

Food

Olives (grown-ups love them)   Yuk!
Sausages
Mini Pizzas
Those mini scotch-eggy things
Extra chocolatey biscuits
Dippy stuff to dip breadsticks in
Breadsticks
Sausage rolls
Jelly babies →
Jelly beans
Jelly to have with ice cream
Normal crisps
Cheesy ball-type crisps
Spaceman-alien-type crisps
Crisps of any and every flavour
     imaginable to humankind
Chocolate swiss roll cakes

How to Come Up with a Theme

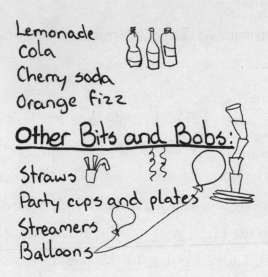

Lemonade
Cola
Cherry soda
Orange fizz

Other Bits and Bobs:

Straws
Party cups and plates
Streamers
Balloons

'I suppose we ought to get some of those doggy chocolates and bones and chews in the shape of shoes and things for the dogs?' I suggested.

'Good idea,' said Molly, nodding seriously and noting down those items on her list. 'In fact there are so many cool treats you can buy for dogs these days – like those weird red balls you can fill with biscuits so that the dogs can roll them around and get the biscuits out.'

'Oh yeah! Doggy biscuits!' I cried. 'Write

down "All manner of shape, colour and size of
dog biscuits".'

May I suggest
'extra-large'?

'And what about a cake for April?' Molly asked.

'And one for Honey!' I cried, getting quite
over-excitical. I loved going to the pet shop and
looking at all the treats for pooches – and now I
had a Budget to go and buy loads of them!

'It might be fun to make some decorations,'
Molly suggested, tapping her pencil against her
teeth. 'We should probably put "card" and "pens"
on the shopping list just in case.'

'Yes,' I agreed. 'We could cut out paw-print
patterns and stick them on the walls and windows.
And maybe make some of those little flags on
strings?'

'Bunting,' said Molly.

How to Come Up with a Theme

'What?' I said, puzzled.

'That's what those little flags on strings are called,' said Molly impatiently.

I decided to ignore her know-it-all manner and move on. 'By the way, I don't think we should tell April about the super brainwave of having dogs at the party.'

Molly nodded in a DECISIVE way and tapped her notebook with her pencil. 'I absolutely and positively agree with you,' she said. 'If this party is a surprise, we should not actually tell her about any of the details of it anyway, should we?'

'But we will have to tell *someone* to get April to the party otherwise she won't come and then it would be a surprise party without her, which would not be much fun or indeed much of a surprise,' I pointed out.

Molly shook her head in a sad and sorry-for-me way and said, 'Honestly, Summer, you can be quite a few sandwiches short of the full

picnic sometimes you know. You will have to tell
NICK of course.'

I was muddled up with excitement and was
not thinking in a straight line. 'But how do I tell
Nick without April overhearing or finding out in
some way?' I said.

Molly said, 'Hmmm,' thoughtfully.

Then her eyes went very wide and shiny and
she beamed a big large smile and put her finger in
the air as though she had just had a EUREKA
moment, which our teacher told us once is an
Ancient Greek word for saying she had had
the most brilliant idea, and she said, 'We will
AMBUSH him at work!'

Can I come?
I love an ambush.

6

How to Progress
a Party Plan

'**D**o you think maybe we should tell *Nick*
about the puppy part of it?' Molly
asked later on while we were having a drink in
the kitchen as a break from our brainstorming.
Brainstorming is thirsty-making work.

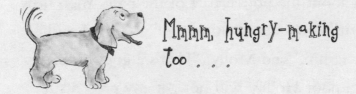

Mmmm, hungry-making
too . . .

'I don't know,' I said. I wasn't sure whether Nick
would be against the idea or not.

'Maybe it will be more of a surprise if we
do not tell him any of the details of the party at

all,' Molly said. 'Now I come to think of it, your mum should be Kept in the Dark too, in case she Spills the Beans.'

'What nonsense are you going on about?' I asked. 'We cannot have the party in the dark, and as for giving people beans to eat—'

'I meant that your mum might by mistake tell April about the surprise if we give her too many details,' Molly explained.

'Ah,' I said. 'I suppose that's right. They are always talking together on the phone about everything. But what about Nick? If we don't tell him about the pooch part of the party then how will he know about bringing Custard?' I said.

'Hmm,' said Molly. 'That's a good point. Also, poor Honey will not get any presents if people do not know that it is her birthday too.'

Whimper

'Honey does not need presents – there will be lots of pooches to play with and lots of doggy treats, and that is all that Honey wants,' I said. Honestly, considering Molly was now a dog-owner-type person, she could be quite weird about what a dog's Essential Needs in Life could be.

Well, actually I wouldn't say no to a present . . .

'Do you know, I've had an astoundly excellent idea about Custard,' I continued. It was truly amazing how many BRAIN-FLASHABLE moments I seemed to be having these days. 'I can invite him as a kind of DECOY, in other words, if Nick and April come round here with Custard, that will make everything seem totally normal as if they are just coming round for tea like they always do! April will not suspect a thing.'

Molly nodded and pulled her mouth down in

an I-am-impressed sort of expression.

Mum came into the
kitchen. 'How's the party-
planning going?' she asked, as
she turned to put the kettle on.

'We-ell,' I said, in a long-
drawn-out and ponder-ish
tone. And then I told her
our thoughts about the
Decoy.

'Mmm,' said Mum.
'I'm not sure about that.
We don't really want Custard *and*
Honey here if we're going to have
a houseful of guests, do we?'

'Oh yes, yes we do!' I said, rather over-hastily.

'Summer is absolutely right,' Molly said. I
gave her a grateful look. 'It will mean that April
will not suspect a thing, as she and Nick always
come round with Custard. They never leave him

at home when they usually come, do they?'

'No-o,' said Mum in a faltering fashion.
She was looking a bit anxious, which made her
forehead even more wrinkly than it was supposed
to be for a woman of her age.

'So we have decided that we will ambush
Nick at work,' Molly went on, 'to tell him about
the party. I'm sure he won't mind that, will he?
Maybe we should take Honey or Titch with us
so that the other people in the vet's think that we
have a proper appointment,' she suggested. Then
she paused and added anxiously, 'Unless you think
he might make us pay for bringing the dogs?'

I glanced at Mum to see if she had any useful
suggestions to add to the conversation. She didn't.
She was actually biting in her lips as if she was
trying not to laugh, for some reason.

'Ahem!' she said squeakily. 'I don't think you
need to take the dogs. And Nick wouldn't charge
us anyway.'

'OH!' said Molly, in a sort of offended manner. 'So you get special family treatment, do you? I don't think that is very fair for all the other patients.'

Well, I am a special case . . .

Mum gave a sort of snorty laugh and then suggested that if we saw Nick we could ask him to help with the guest list. Then she told us to excuse her, because she had to go and do something she'd just forgotten she had to do.

I decided to draw the conversation back to the party as we were getting Off The Point. 'Listen,' I said in a calm and collected-ish tone of speaking. 'Let's go to his vet place straight away after school tomorrow when we have broken up for the holidays. There is no way April will be there as her office job does not finish until at least half past five.'

Molly was still glaring at me but I made my face all sweet and innocent-ish and just said, 'Oh, sorry, is tomorrow not a convenient day for you? Never mind, I am not bothered if I have to go on my own to ask him.'

'Oh no, you mustn't go on your own,' Molly said, immediately sounding worried and concerned. 'I am sure that I can make it and it doesn't matter if you don't want me to bring Titch. It might make him over-excited and rather Impossible to Deal with, anyway.'

So that is what we did the next afternoon. It was the kind of day that Mum describes as GLORIOUS! in a smiley, beamy voice as if she is about to break into song like people do in musicals. The birds were singing and the sun was shining and the clouds were white and poofy (which are my favourite kind of clouds as they are all different shapes and you can have fun staring up at them and trying to find pictures in them. Once I found a pig and another time I saw the whole entire map of the British Isles and another time there was a dog's head that I am absolutely convinced and certain was the same shape as Honey's head).

Nope. I'm far more Beautiful.

I don't know if it was the weather or if it was the fact that we had just finished school for the term (hurrah and double hurrah!) or if it was that we were fizzing with excitement about the secret party, but Molly and I were actually skipping down the road to the vet's.

'Do you think Nick will be as OVER-THE-TOP-OF-THE-MOON about the secret party idea as we are?' I chirruped to Molly.

How to Progress a Party Plan

'I don't know,' said Molly, pausing mid-skip as she thought about this, which meant that I crashed into her as I lost my balance when I turned to see why she had stopped and sort of toppled sideways. 'Ow!' Molly said angrily.

'"Ow", yourself!' I said, rubbing my own arm. 'Why have you stopped?'

Molly said grumpily, 'Cos your question stopped me completely literally in my mid-tracks. It has made me wonder something.'

'Oh,' I said. 'And what is that?'

Molly took a deep breath and then said, 'Well, what if Nick has already thought up a super-romantic and ultra-dreamy date for April's first birthday as his wife?'

'Urgh!' I said. I didn't mean to say that. It just slipped out.

Molly rolled her eyes and said, 'Honestly, Summer. You are allowed to be romantic when you are married, you know. Just because you have got married does not mean you have to stop doing romantic things together. In fact, the Agony Uncle in the magazine my mum reads called *Good Housewife* says that you *should* be romantic when you are married, even if you have been married for about fifty years like my parents have, because if you stop being romantic, then that is when The Love Dies.'

It was my turn to roll my eyes mega-hugely now. 'Let's just stop talking about it, can we? It is after all MY sister that I am now imagining being romantic, and it is not an image that I like to have to hold on to in my head, thank you very much. If Nick has made such a **YUCKSOME** plan, he shall simply have to RESCHEDULE it for another occasion, in other words, not on April's birthday.'

How to Progress a Party Plan

Molly laughed and said, 'OK. Race you to the end of the road!'

So that was the end of the conversation about Romantic Things, thank the high heavens above.

7
How to Get Past the Front Desk

Nick was busy when we got there. At least, that is what the beaky-nosed snarly receptionist said when we asked if we could talk to him.

'No,' she said, in the sort of voice which I think is called NASAL, in other words it sounds as though the person is really talking through their nose passages instead of their mouth. And this lady did have an exceptionally ginormous nose, so maybe she did in fact talk with it instead of using the normal manner of human communication.

I thought back to when Felicity Shufflebottom had been working in the surgery.

How to Get Past the Front Desk

(Yes, that is a real name.) She had not been a nice person because she had tried to run off with Nick while he was going out with my sister. Mum said Felicity had Set Her Sights on Nick, which apparently means that she was a very determined woman and had decided that she would get Nick to go out with her, no matter what. Luckily Nick was much too nice and honest and (I hate to say it) too much in LUrrrrrve with April to be distractivated by the strange fluttery-eyed attentions of someone like her, and so everything worked out all right in the end. Nick told Felicity that he could not go out with her because he was in love with April, and to prove it he asked April to marry him, and The Bottom Shuffler (as I secretly like to call her) was so upset when she found out that she stormed out of the vet's in a huff and said she would get a job elsewhere and that would teach Nick 'not to mess with a woman's emotional state', whatever that means.

Puppy Party

Good riddance to her, is what I say. I mean,
April could be pretty unbearable at the best of
times, but while The Bottom Shuffler (aka TBS)
was trying to get her Grip of Iron around Nick,
April was totally and completely impossible to live
with. So I for one was rather a bit relieved when
TBS moved off the scene.

But even if you took all that
PHENOMENAL hoo-ha into consideration, it
had to be said that Felicity Shufflebottom was
at least much nicer than this old beeswax of a
person with a huge beaky nose who Molly and I
were CONFRONTED with that afternoon (and,
believe me, I never thought I would say *that*).

'Fine,' I said, in a strong and purposeful voice.
'If Mr Harris is busy that is all right. We will wait
until he is free.'

'You don't *appear* to have an appointment,'
said Nasal Woman, making a big deal out of
peering at her computer screen and then peering

back at us. 'And you don't *appear* to have an animal with you, either.'

Molly dug me in the ribs and twisted her mouth at me in an I-told-you-so look, but I was not going to be DETERRED, which is a posh way of saying I was not going to be put off.

I pulled my shoulders back and held my head high to make myself look taller and said firmly, 'I do not need an appointment or an animal actually, as Nick Harris is married to my sister and so *technically* I am family.'

Molly sniggered and Nasal Woman arched one eyebrow so high it almost

disappeared into her fringe (something which would have impressed me if I had been in the mood to be impressed, which I was not). Then she started to say, 'That may be, young lady, but I am afraid I have been given strict instructions not to let anyone see the vet without an appoint—'

'Hello, Summer! Oh dear, Honey hasn't got herself into trouble has she? Eaten something she shouldn't have?' It was Nick, who had emerged from his Consulting Room behind Nasal Woman's back, so she had not seen him and was still being HOITY-TOITY with me.

'Hi, Nick!' I said cheerily, ignoring Nasal Woman. She had whirled around and gone red in the face when she had seen that Nick did know me and was in fact pleased to see me.

'What are you doing leaving these girls out here, Penelope?' Nick said. 'You know I'm free at the moment. You should have waved them through.'

How to Get Past the Front Desk

'I – er – aah,' said Nasal Penelope.

'Never mind,' said Nick, waving his hand impatiently. 'Come through, girls. I've only got ten minutes till the next patient.'

We left Nasal Penelope opening and closing her mouth like a goldfish at feeding time and followed Nick into his room.

'So what's up with my beautiful girl then?' Nick said in a weird soppy voice, and looking around as though he had lost something.

'Er, I don't know,' I said, puzzled. 'I would have thought you would have known if there was anything wrong with April seeing as you are now legally her husband and have to live with her all the time—'

Molly nudged me *very* hard in the ribs at this point, which made me shriek, which made Nick burst out laughing, which was not very kind of him, I thought.

'Whatyoudothatfor?' I hissed at Molly, who

was also laughing now.

'You numpty, Nick is asking how *Honey* is, not your sister!' Molly said, between laughs and gasps for breath.

'Oh,' I said, feeling stupid. 'Erm, nothing is up with your beautiful girl. Which is why I have not brought her with me.'

Nick looked puzzled. 'Oh, I see. Is Titch OK, Molly?'

'Yes,' she said quietly before bellowing with laughter again.

'Honestly, Molly,' I said impatiently. 'You said you wanted to come with me to tell Nick all about the party and now you are not being one single ounce of a bit of help. Will you please stop laughing?'

'A party?' said Nick, perking up.

I turned back to him and said, 'Yes. We have come to ask you for some help, as Mum and I thought it would be lovely to have a surprise party for April's birthday and we wanted to ask you to call some friends of hers that you think she would like to come. But the thing which is most important about all this is that you must NOT tell April. Otherwise it will not be a *surprise* party. That is why we have come here to tell you about it instead of ringing you up or coming round to the flat.'

'Aha,' said Nick, nodding. 'I see. Great idea. Of course I'll help.'

'And you'll keep it a secret from April?'

Nick nodded again. 'Yes,' he said, sounding very definite. 'Although . . .' he added, not sounding definite at all.

'What?' I demanded. I was not liking his tone of speaking changing so suddenly like that. '"Although" what?'

Nick looked uncomfortable. 'You know what April's like . . . she is very good at finding things out. I mean, I will do my best to keep things under cover, but I'm just saying I can't promise she won't discover what we're up to!'

'You jolly well better had,' I said, putting on the same voice I had used for Nasal Penelope outside at the reception desk.

Nick chewed his bottom lip as though he was going to start laughing again. 'Yes, sir!' he said, doing a comical salute as though I was the captain of a ship or an army-type commander person.

'Oh! And the most important thing of all,' I said, remembering the conversation I had had earlier with Mum and Molly, 'is that you need to get April around to our house – I mean, *my* house – oh, you know! – without her knowing why she is coming round.'

How to Get Past the Front Desk

'What?' said Nick confusedly.

Molly gave a whooshy sigh and stepped forward a bit to get Nick's attention. 'What Summer means is, the party's at her place, but because it's a surprise, you have to bring April round there on the day without her knowing what she's going round for. You'll have to make up some kind of story about her mum wanting to give her a present face to face or wanting to see her darling daughter on her special day or something like that. I'm sure you can think of something. Maybe you could bring Custard just like when you are coming for a normal Run Off the Mill cup of tea. Custard can be your Decoy.'

'My what?' said Nick.

'If you bring Custard,' I said, glaring at Molly for making things worse, 'then April will definitely not guess it is a party she is going to, as who would bring their puppy to a party? Hahahahaaaaa!' I gave a very **over-the-top** dramatical nervous laugh when I said this last bit, which was severely unfortunate as it meant that I did not exactly sound realistical in my reasoning.

Molly was glaring at *me* now.

'Ri–ight,' said Nick, in a hesitating tone. 'Well, I suppose that makes sense.'

I let myself breathe again, and Molly's glare faded. 'Great,' I said quickly. 'So that's all arranged then. Molly and I will do the food and the decorations and all that. All you have to do is invite the people you think April would like to have as her guests and make sure you keep it a secret.'

Nick nodded. 'Guest list and invites. Right. Leave it with me,' he said.

'Thanks.' I turned to leave the surgery before he could ask me any awkward questions that might make anything go wrong with the plans. But I was not quick enough.

'Er, Summer,' said Nick.

How to Get Past the Front Desk

'Mmm?' I said, only half turning back.

'Are you sure your mum will be OK about having Custard and Honey around when there are so many people in the house?'

'Absolutely one hundred and ten per cent,' I said, crossing my fingers. 'The more dogs and people, the totally much more merrier it will be.'

And then I really did leave, dragging Molly swiftly behind me.

8
How to Work to a Budget

Molly, Frank Gritter and I were in the park with our pooches, which is quite possibly one of the best ways of spending an Easter holiday day, in my opinion. This is mainly because being in the park with pooches is a pretty cool thing in itself, but also because all our three dogs are related! Frank's dog Meatball (I know, don't ask) is Honey's mum and Honey is Titch's mum!

Molly loved it when all three dogs got together too, although if she had had her way, she would not have had Frank there as well, as they were not what you would call On Good Terms most of the time. But she was just about willing

to put up with him for the sake of
our three dogs.

I'm out with Mum and Grandma!

Molly was doing her best to ignore Frank by
sitting on a park bench with her Notebook
of Outstanding Beauty on her lap, scribbling
furiously. Frank was completely OBLIVIOUS
to the fact that he was being ignored and was
throwing sticks for the dogs. He was also telling
me an extremely stupid but actually very funny
joke about a fruit sweet saying it did not want to
be friends with a mint sweet because it was
'really menthol'.

I knew I
should not
encourage
Frank
when he was

in such a daft mood, as he was quite likely to become Too Big for His Boots, in other words, start showing off in an impossible and irritating manner, but I could not help thinking it was funny as it was truly a very good joke. So I was laughing uproariously and finding it vastly hard to breathe like a normal person.

Molly was NOT AMUSED, as Queen Victoria used to say.

'Will you two shut up?' she said, snappishly. 'I am trying to brainstorm some ideas for the party, and you are not being any help whatsoever. Honestly, I think if I did not put in all this effort, there would not BE a party. Do you realize, Summer—?'

'OK!' I said, stifling another giggle. Then something occurred to me. 'What exactly *are* you planning at the moment? I thought we had finished brainstorming on the food and decorations front? And Nick is doing invitations . . .'

How to Work to a Budget

'Ahem,' Molly coughed in a way that said I-have-thought-of-something-you-have-not.

'Here it comes – another marvellous masterly Molly-style plan,' Frank whispered, threatening to make me giggle all over again.

'Mmffgh!' I squeaked, biting my cheeks in.

'AHEM!' Molly coughed a bit more loudly. 'I believe you have Overlooked the Obvious.'

'Eh?' I said.

'There is the small problem of the *puppy* part of this whole party,' she said, making herself sound very important indeed.

'Why is it a problem?' I asked. 'We have made a list of the food. What else do we need to do?'

'Yeah,' said Frank. 'It's not like you need a *plan* for having a few dogs round. It's no big deal. People come, they bring their dogs, the dogs play – probably outside otherwise it'll be Havoc with a capital H—'

Puppy Party

Havoc is my middle name . . .

'Which is *exactly* what we want to avoid, Mr Oh-So-Clever-And-Pleased-With-Yourself!' Molly butted in. 'We do not want Summer's mum – or even worse, April – freaking out about the dogs running around all over the place and then telling us we have done a rubbish job of this party and that all the dogs must go home at once.'

'So what is *your* solution then?' I asked.

Frank and I exchanged puzzled and unimpressed glances, which involved us making our mouths go sneery and raising our eyebrows at each other. Except that Frank only ever raises one

eyebrow, as he thinks it makes him look more sophisticateder and James Bond-ish.

Molly's eyes popped out of her head and she said, 'Well if you can be bothered to listen to me for one second instead of giggling in a rather immature manner at all HIS pathetic jokes . . .' She paused and stared at us SCARILY AND FLARILY like teachers do when they are waiting for the class to calm down.

Frank and I managed to avoid catching each other's eye again.

Molly took a big dramatical breath and said, 'Right. So, what I was thinking was: if we make sure we buy the most delicious dog treats on the planet, we can use them to control the pooches. You know, Summer, it's like when you are training your dog to be a highly obedient and well-behaved hound. You give them food when they are good, don't you?'

I nodded a bit uncertainly. I did not want the

party to turn into a huge dog-training session. I had done enough of those in my lifetime to last me, well, a lifetime.

Molly rolled her eyes impatiently and said, 'So, it's simple! We can play games with the dogs which involve them getting a yummy treat when they do as they are told. Like we could play "musical pups" and get them to sit when the music stops. They will do anything we ask to get their paws on the treats, especially if we come up with an amazing menu of food which is specifically ⊼AI⊾ORED to suit doggy appetites.'

'What does *that* mean?' Frank chortled. 'Are you going to sew all the snacks out of fabric and stuff?'

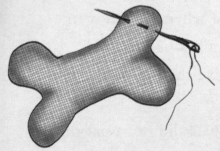

'That is not what I mean, no,' said Molly, her face going a bit purply red. 'But if you are too busy with your *girlfriend*

here to want to know what I am planning, then that is fine.'

'**ooOOOOOooo!** No need to get your knickers in a tangle!' Frank said, which was probably not the most helpful thing he might have said.

'We might have to think carefully about games for the dogs,' I said quickly, changing the subject to stop Molly from going into Full-On Strop Mode (and also because I privately thought the game 'musical pups' sounded nonsensical and rubbish). 'I mean, we can't just make them up on the spot – we should plan them in advance. What do you think, Frank? Have you got any ideas for this party?'

Molly gave me yet another scary glare, then she flicked her eyes quickly at Frank and then back at me. I read the Coded Signal at once, which was 'Don't get HIM involved'.

'What's your budget?' Frank asked casually. I

smiled gratefully at him. Molly likes talking about all things maths-related.

'Fifty pounds,' said Molly proudly.

'Fifty pounds!' Frank hooted. 'Fifty quid's not going to get you far! How many guests are you buying for?'

I changed my grateful smile to a distinctively ungrateful GLOWER.

'We're not sure yet,' I muttered. 'But probably about thirty human guests and then possibly four or five dogs.'

Frank spluttered with snorty laughter. 'Get real!' he said. 'How are you going to afford dog food and treats as well as the stuff for the humans?'

Yeah, don't forget — I'm a growing pupsicle!

'The thing is, FRANK,' Molly said sourly. 'I

116

don't recall asking you for YOUR opinion on
how to work to a budget.'

I felt a churning panicky sensation start up in
my tummy. Molly was right: we had not asked
Frank about that. But the more I thought about
it, the more I realized that he was probably right.
We did not have enough money for everything
we had planned! But how was I going to get
Molly to see this now that she was On A Roll
with her organizational skills? She was not likely
to want to discuss CUTBACKS at this stage, in
other words, she was not going to take anything
off that list, and especially not in front of Frank.

So I suggested that we call the dogs and go
home.

'Yeah, I've got to go anyway,' Frank said.
'I've got footy practice.'

'Thank the highest heavens for that,' said
Molly under her breath, but not so far under it
that we couldn't hear her.

117

'Don't miss me too much!' he called over his shoulder, as he grabbed hold of Meatball's collar and put her lead on.

Molly narrowed her eyes at him and stuck her tongue out.

On the way back from the park Molly rattled on and on and did not let me get a word in edgeways, frontways or any which way about my money worries.

'We could do the games for the dogs in the garden to make sure they run off all their energy and, as well as the treats, we could give them prizes, like a new collar or a cuddly toy or something!' she was saying. 'That will stop the dogs causing havoc *and* it will keep them out of the way of the boring grown-ups.'

But I wasn't really listening to all the Finer Points, in other words the details of her ideas, because, to be honest, the panicky feeling was now growing so strongly in my stomach that I was listening instead to the worrying thoughts going round and round inside my brain.

Molly didn't seem to notice how PREOCCUPIED and anxious I was. When I left her and Titch at their front door, she said cheerily: 'Oh wow, I'm soooo excited about this pooch party! I'm going to go and do some more research right now. See you later!'

'Hmm,' I said, and waved distractivatedly as I walked away from her place.

Once I was back home, I started deeply trying to think of a way to get Mum to give me some more money. I decided to do what I usually do in such a situation which is to think out a Very Carefully Planned Conversation in my head before I actually speak a word aloud. And this was what I planned:

'Dearest Mum, you have been soooo amazingly generous to give me fifty whole pounds to spend on April's birthday party and it really is a lot of money, but did you know that I have been doing a lot of Research about how much parties cost, and there is a bit of a problem with Inflation, in other words, things for parties cost more than they did when you were young! I know that this is very unfair and stupid of the government, but as an Individual on my own I cannot do anything about Inflation, and I am starting to get worried that April is not going to have much of a party. So I was wondering if you could help out by perhaps maybe **inflating** the amount of money I am allowed to spend. Thank you so much and very sincerely.'

I was quite pleased with this speech, and I thought it would be even better if I produced some figures and things on a piece of paper to show that I had done my maths. I grabbed a pad of paper and began to scribble away.

How to Work to a Budget

'Hello, Summer!' Mum called, coming into the kitchen and finding me with a pile of screwed-up paper and what I expect was a very worried look on my face. 'What's up? You haven't got homework to do, have you? It's the holidays!'

'No, no I am just a bit concerned about Inflation,' I said. Oh dearie goodness, that was not exactly how I had planned to start the conversation.

'Tell me about it,' said Mum, kicking off her shoes and sitting down with a heavy sigh. 'I popped to the shops to get a few bits for tea tonight, and it came to twice what I thought it would! I honestly feel as though I might just as well stand from the upstairs window and throw ten-pound notes out into the street some days.'

I frowned in puzzlement. Surely that would not be a good way to save money?

Mum sighed again and rubbed her forehead in a tired and exhaustified fashion. 'So what's a young girl like you doing worrying about inflation?' she asked, smiling weakly.

'Well, it's because of April's party,' I began, looking as innocently sweet and lovely as I could by making my eyes wide and putting my head on one side.

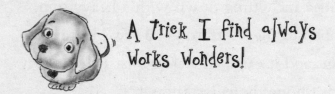 A trick I find always works wonders!

'Yes?' said Mum, in a suspicious-sounding tone.

'Erm, can I have some more money as the budget is not working?' I said in a rush.

And Mum looked me squarely in the eyes, her mouth set in a grimly serious manner and asked, 'Why?'

How to Work to a Budget

Oh blow, I could not tell her about needing extra food and possibly now prizes just for the dogs, could I? 'Erm, well, food, as you have just said, is sooooo over-the-top EXTORTIONATE in its pricing these days, and then there's the decorations, and we have not even thought about drinks and—'

'Oh, don't worry about the drinks!' Mum said cheerily. 'I was going to get them. The adults might want wine, and you can hardly buy that. You're only buying crisps and things, aren't you?'

I nodded weakly.

'Exactly! I hardly think a few packets of crisps and some balloons and streamers are going to cost you more than fifty pounds. I don't suppose we'll have more than thirty people anyway.'

Well, that's that then, I thought grimly. But I smiled and said, 'OK!' in as Up-Beat a voice as I could manage.

Puppy Party

Now I would have to have a very well-planned conversation in my head about how I was going to break the news to Molly that we did not have enough money for the pooches.

I don't like the sound of that.

9

How to Come Up with Option Two

I called round at Molly's later on while Mum was battling with the Ironing Pile. The Ironing Pile was making her mood worse and worse as it is her least favouritest chore in the universe of chores, so when I said I was going round to Molly's after tea, she just muttered at me and told me not to come home late.

I felt utterly DESpAIRING to THE DEpτHS oF MY BooτS by the time I got to my Best Friend's house.

Even the sight of little Mr Titch (as I sometimes like to call him) running up and down the hallway with his most loved cuddly in his

125

jaws, shaking his head from side to side like an insane maniac, was not enough to lift my mood.

Grrrr. I am a toughie. I am gonna be the champion of this cuddly, you'll see.

Luckily Molly told me that she had been getting her Thinking Cap on about the party (which does not mean that she has a special hat to wear for when she is pondering about things, as that would just be plain daft, it means that she had been doing a lot of in-depth planning and problem-solving). This made me feel slightly more hopeful.

Until, that is, Molly said, 'I have been working on some calculations, Summer, and I can very safely tell you that there is No Way Ho-Zay that we can get all the stuff that we need with the very small amount of money that your mum has given you, so I am afraid we are going to have to ask for

How to Come Up with Option Two

an Increase of the Budget.'
She said this with her nose
a little bit in the air and
her clipboard up high as
though she was a teacher
on a school trip, ticking off
who was on the bus.

I wanted to say, 'So
Frank was right?' But I felt
too DEFLATED to say
anything mean like that, so instead I said, 'Oh?'

'Yes,' said Molly, tapping her pen against
her clipboard. Then she peered at me in a
CONSPIRATORIAL way and beckoned me to
follow her quickly up the stairs. Titch followed
with his cuddly, even though Strictly Speaking
he is not permitted to go upstairs. But for once
Molly seemed to have more important things on
her mind than the extremely strict Cook Family
Rulebook.

127

Puppy Party

I take my chances while I can in this place!

Then once we were all safely inside in her room with the door closed, Molly said in a low voice: 'I did a HACK into my mum's Supermarket Online Shopping list and I pretended to do a shop of all the things I think we need for the party so that I could see how much it would cost.'

'Wow!' I breathed. I had to admit, this was pretty impressive of her. I would never have thought of finding out like that. I would probably have gone around the supermarket with a paper list of shopping and a calculator and written it all down and then I would probably have been thrown out of the store for Wasting Precious Time when it became obvious to the store manager that I was not actually going to buy one single item.

But Molly is much cleverer than me, which is why even though she can be the bossiest boot in the boot rack, she is also a rather exceptionally good person to be Best Friends with.

'That is amazing, Molly,' I said.

Molly went pink with pleasure at my admiring-ness of her, and nodded. 'I know,' she said.

'So, can you show me the hack?' I asked.

Molly put on her serious face again. 'I am afraid I can't cos Mum is on the computer at the moment,' she told me. 'But I can tell you, the shopping bill came out to be a lot more than the amount your mum has given you.'

'How much more, Molly?' I said despairingly. 'I have to tell you that I have already asked Mum for an increase of the budget, and she has said NO.'

'Well, we are going to have to find the money from somewhere. Fifty pounds does not go far these days,' she said importantly, not answering my question, I noticed.

'Molly,' I tried again. 'How much—?'

Molly waved a hand at me, looking slightly

pink for some reason: 'We really do need to Think Outside the Box, in other words, we need a plan. SO!' she cried, pointing one finger in the air. 'This is what we must do – and there are Two Options,' she said, putting another finger in the air and dropping her pen.

Mmm–mmm!

A nice chewy stick-thing.

I waited. By now I was actually a bit struck with awe at Molly's mega-organizational mood. And I was very glad that she was full of ideas and obviously not feeling as desperational as I was.

'Option One,' she said, 'is that we do not buy everything, which is obviously not an option at all otherwise the party will be completely useless—'

'BUT—!' I cried.

Molly interrupted. 'And Option Two is – we find a Masterly Plan to *earn* some extra money!'

How to Come Up with Option Two

She clasped her clipboard to her and beamed
a big satisfied smile.

'Huh?' I said.

Molly frowned. '*Huh?*' she said. 'Is that all
you can say when I have gone to so much trouble
to work all this out for you?'

I said, 'But you have not worked out
anything! We cannot just "earn money" like
that.' I clicked my fingers. 'We are quite young
children, in case you hadn't noticed. How are we
supposed to get a job in real life?'

Molly chewed her lip and looked a tiny
bit worried and un-Molly-like for about one
nanosecond. And then her eyes twinkled and she
said, 'Aha! We can wear a disguise and pretend
we are older than we are and I can fake a letter
on my dad's office notepaper to Employers
everywhere to say that we are marvellous at doing
jobs, and then they will all employ us and pay us
lots of money.'

Puppy Party

'STOP! STOP!' I shouted, waving my arms in the air. I was now feeling rather un-admiring of my best friend who seemed to be losing the plot ultra-fast. 'This is just about the craziest of crazy plans you have ever come up with, Molly Cook. In fact, it is even more crazier than my sister's plan for wearing fake beards around the house when Honey was freaked out by Nick's beard.'

'AHA!' Molly shouted, waving her arms in the air now, and narrowly missing my head with her clipboard. 'I am glad you reminded me of the beards, Summer! We can use them as part of our disguise.'

Things are getting exciting now!

'NOOOOOO!' I cried. Had the world gone completely insane and Around the Twist all of a sudden? Or was I trapped inside a particularly weirdo and frankly rather nasty **NIGHTMARE** which if I didn't wake up from soon would muck up all the systems of my brain forever?

Molly had her Extremely Cross face on, so I panicked and said, 'What I mean is, I have a Very Strong Feeling that April got rid of those beards quite a long time ago. Maybe there is another way that we could earn some money . . .'

At that moment Titch stopped jumping around for once and put his paw on my lap. Then he looked up at me with an expression I recognized from my own gorgeous Honey which I think said: when-are-you-going-to-stop-chin-waggling-and-take-me-for-a-walk? In other words he put his head on one side in his most cutesome pose and let out a little whine most pleadingly.

I was hoping for a snack, actually.
That stick-thing didn't taste so good.

133

And that is when I had one of those ultra-sonic brainflashes of the kind that make your head go **fizz!** and your face go **beam!** and your legs go springy with excitement.

'That's it!' I cried, leaping up and dancing around the room, which resulted in Titch becoming very jumpy again indeed. 'I have got it, By Jove!' (I have always thought 'By Jove' was a rather fantabulous way of expressing excitement.)

Molly was looking rather a bit quizzical, but she did not try to get me to shut up so I carried on: 'We can earn money AND have fun!'

'Oh? How's that then?' said Molly.

At that point I turned very dramatical and whirled to face her like a superhero in a big cloak (although I was not of course actually wearing one myself at that PRECISE moment) and announced in a 'taa-daaaaa'-type way of speaking: 'We can advertise around the neighbourhood to say that we are available to WALK PEOPLE'S

How to Come Up with Option Two

DOGS for them before and after school and we can charge them something like one pound a go.'

Molly shook her head violently. I felt my heart go skidding down into my socks so fast I thought I might be sick. How could she not see how utterly brilliant my plan was? Even Mr Titchical was on the exact same length of wave as me. He was bouncing up and putting his paws on Molly's legs just as if he was trying to convince her of the intelligence and wonderment of my brainflash.

I'll help! I luuuurve walking with other poochicals!

Molly shushed Titch and settled him down and then took what I thought was a whole eternity patting him with a deeply thoughtful look on her face.

Then she turned to me and said, 'If we are

going to do this then we should at least ask for
two pounds every time.'

And then she arched one eyebrow at me in a
devilish sort of a way and I grinned.

'Molly Cook, you are an evil genius,' I said.
'Two pounds it is.'

10
How to Cope with an Abundance of Pooches

The problem with advertising for dog-walking services around the neighbourhood was that I had not realized quite how many dogs there were, or how keen people were NOT to walk their own dogs. Now, you may think that this was not a problem at all, as we were after all quite desperational for money for the party, so surely having lots and lots of pooches to walk would be a truly marvellous thing.

But how exactly are you supposed to manage with your *own* pooch (who is, frankly, rather a BoISʏERoUS and BUMpʏIoUS animal at the very best of times) . . .

What are you saying?
I'm offended.

. . . *and* hold on to one Dalmatian, one
dachshund, one beagle and one fluffy thing
(which might possibly have been a poodle, but
if so was quite definitely the hairiest, whitest,
PERFUMIEST one of its kind that *I*
have ever seen in real life or even
in a book) *all at the same time?*

I can tell you that it was a
Sight to Behold: me with five different leads and
five different poochicals, all pulling and running in
different directions, some of them wanting to race
each other and some of them wanting to chase
each other and some of them wanting to sniff
each other's bottoms and some of them (especially
the poodley one) trying to get as far away from
the others as is doggedly possible.

Of course, you may well ask, 'Why on

earth did you not give a couple of these canine
creatures to your Bestest Friend, Molly Cook, to
look after?' Well, I will tell you why, dear reader.
Because SHE WAS HOLDING ON TO FIVE
OTHER POOCHES, THAT'S WHY!!!

'Summer!' Molly squealed, as a greyhound,
a wolfhound,
a foxhound, a
cocker spaniel
and a springer
spaniel pulled

her arms in five different directions, wound their leads around her legs and sent her flying along the pavement at fifty miles an hour. 'I think this is possibly the most daftest idea you have ever had in the history of the world's most daftest ideas!'

It was not a nice thing to say, but I have to say that I agreed with her.

We just about managed to get our pooches to the park without any disasters (unless you count all ten of them pooping on the pavement in Quick Succession, meaning that all our poop bags were used up before we had even got to the end of our road), then we opened the park gate and let them off the lead so that they could have a good run around and LET OFF STEAM.

It was just as the greyhound went zooming into the bushes way over in the furthest corner of the park that I thought to myself, 'I wonder if that dog is as well-trained as Honey, because if it is not, we will never get it back, and then I will have to buy the owner a new dog, and that will mean that I will have Zero Money and I really will *have* to leave school and get a job.'

Just as the panic was beginning to rise right up inside me, a familiar voice broke into my nightmarish thoughts with the words:

'Hi, Summer. You look as though you've lost something.'

Typical. It was the one and only know-it-all boy, Frank Gritter, who even though he can make me laugh with his DER-BRAIN sense of humour, can be especially annoying when it comes to him making out that he is a vastly more intelligenter and Superior Being to me, a Mere Girl. In other words, he was totally and completely *not* the person I was wanting to come across in the park on the very day that I had decided to take five dogs for a walk and then lose them all in the bushes.

He had his lovely dog Meatball with him

141

which was something, I suppose. She was always all right even when Frank was not.

 Charmed, I'm sure.

'So, have you? Lost something, I mean?' Frank said. He wiggled his eyebrows and grinned cheekily in that way which always seems to have the effect of making me smile even when I am In A Deep Dark Mood and really want to Take It Out on someone, i.e. Frank.

'Yes, well, I suppose in a way I sort of have,' I said.

'Then why are you smiling?' Frank asked, in a teasing fashion.

I bit in the sides of my cheeks. 'You know why, Frank Gritter! It is because of your ridiculous caterpillar-like eyebrows. Stop it!' I demanded, as he began wiggling them so much I thought they might at some point fly off his

actual head. 'I am actually in the middle of a Very
Serious Situation of a Lost and Found nature and
if you were really my friend you would leave me
alone and not get in the way by acting in such
a clownishly unhelpful manner!' I was trying to
sound serious and to make myself frown, but sadly
it was not working.

Frank bit in the sides of *his* cheeks and also
frowned in an attempt to look serious. 'When did
you last see the suspect?' he asked, in a detective-
ish way, one hand stroking his
chin thoughtfully, the other
propping it up across his body
in a Rather Ridiculous Pose.

'There is no suspect!' I
howled. I had totally given
in to the giggling now.

'Excuse *me*, Summer.'

Oh dearie goodness
me, it was Molly and she

was going to want to know why I was having
a hilarious giggling fit when I should have been
Controlling My Dogs.

'Why exactly are you having a hilarious
giggling fit when you should be Controlling Your
Dogs?' she asked.

I glanced in the direction of the bushes in time
to see ten tails disappear into the undergrowth.

Molly's face was what her mum would call
A Picture, which is a way of saying that she was
such a thundery storm cloud of crossness
with steam almost literally spurting out of her
nostrils like an annoyed dragon, that Frank and I
could not help ourselves. We exchanged a look
that said Ooooh-look-who's-being-a-bossy-boots,
and then we simply DISSOLVED.

How to Cope with an Abundance of Pooches

Molly huffed and said, 'Well, I am glad you find this whole Palaver so over-the-top hysterical, but I personally think it is rather anxious-making that between us, we have lost TEN dogs.'

At that point, my own gorgeous poochical came racing towards us out of nowhere and practically bowled us over in her enthusiasm to say 'hello' to Meatball.

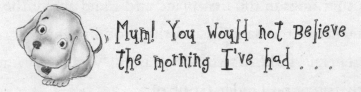 Mum! You would not believe the morning I've had . . .

The two Labradors chased each other round and round and Honey jumped on top of Meatball and put her paws around her as if she was really giving her a cuddle.

We're having a mother
and daughter moment.

It was actually quite cute to look at, and made me
think about family, and then **that made my
mind go round in a loop** and I remembered
why I was supposed to be looking after all these
other dogs in the first place and I said above the
racket of the barking and the shouting and the
general HULLABALOO: 'Listen! We have to get
the situation Under Control.'

'You don't say!' Molly muttered between
extremely gritted teeth.

'Well, I could help?' said Frank.

'WHAT?' Molly and I said in UNISON.

I was not believing what I was hearing with
my own ears: Frank Gritter was offering to help
us out of his own kindness and the freedom of his
own will?

'Yeah, course I'll help,' he said, his face all smooth with innocence. Then, just as I thought I might actually faint from the shock of this moment, his eyes went glinty and his mouth twisted into a menacing smile and he added: 'For a small fee.'

'HUMPF!' I cried, and crossed my arms very violently in front of my chest. I was no longer feeling very giggly or amused.

'HUMPF indeed!' Molly added, doing the same. 'Come on, Summer. We do not need the help of a stinky boy who is only interested in taking money away from us. We can do this on our own.'

'This I have to see,' said Frank, his menacing smile growing more eviller by the minute.

Molly had run off in the direction of the bushes and was shouting all the dogs' names and frantically waving her arms.

Frank looked at me and shrugged. 'As I say,

I'm willing to help, but it'll cost you.'

'No Way, Ho-Zay!' I protested.

'OK, well, better be off then,' Frank said, turning away from me.

ARGH! This was becoming a total nightmare. 'Wait!' I cried. 'Come back!'

Frank turned round slowly and said, 'So, how's about we call it a fiver if I get the dogs for you?'

I closed my eyes and breathed in and out a bit to force myself to sound in control. Then I opened my eyes and said calmly, 'Well, much as I would like your help, Frank Gritter, I cannot possibly pay you that much as I happen to have enough money worries as it is.' Then I turned away from him very ABRUPTLY, in other words fast, because a lump had inconveniently appeared in my throat and I was in danger of letting a tear or two spill out of my eyes. Everything was going about as wrong as it could go.

And it was about to go wronger, I thought, as

How to Cope with an Abundance of Pooches

Meatball and Honey had decided to follow Molly into the bushes.

Hide and seek!

I whirled round and shouted, 'Honey – NO!'

Our favourite game!

Too late. The pooches had whizzed off at the speed of light. I walked right up to Frank and fixed him with my scariest look. I knew I probably was behaving like a raving loony, my eyes streaky and leaky, my face bright red and blotchy (which always happens when I'm upset and which never looks good with my shade of auburn hair). But things had got too serious to worry about any of that.

'Are you going to help or not?' I almost screamed.

Puppy Party

Frank looked a tiny bit astounded, but then he raised his eyes to the skies and then spent a lot of time examining his nails and making quite a huge deal out of waiting patiently to see what would happen next.

What happened next was that Molly came running back from the bushes, her hair all sticky-uppy and her face red and sweaty and her eyebrows cross and frowny. 'OK,' she said, through teeth that were clenched so hard together they might have actually cracked a bit. 'If you are such a fantabulous dog-trainer-type-person and know-it-all boy, why don't you get them all back, Frank Gritter?'

I held my breath.

'My pleasure,' he said, grinning his rather grubby face off.

And he put two fingers into his mouth and Let Forth the most SUPERSONIC WHISTLE I have ever heard in my entire life. And, let me tell you, I have heard quite a few whistles since being a dog-owner-type person, because you often hear people in the park whistling to their dogs. But this was a whistle which I think you could probably describe as being In A League Of Its Own. It was the kind of whistle which those shepherd-types use when they are rounding up their sheep with their highly trained sheepdogs.

Fortunately the bunch of highly *untrained* dogs we were in charge of were quite obviously impressed by Frank's amazing whistle too, as they all came running at once and charging towards us. Unfortunately it did also have the rather undesirous effect of making quite a few other dogs come running towards us as well.

Someone call?

151

Is there food?

It was actually a huge
KERFUFFLE and we did get a
bit trampled on by all the dogs chasing
each other and us and barking and jumping up.
But in the kerfuffle I was able to grab a couple of
collars and I shouted at Frank and Molly to do the
same and in the end we did manage at least to get
leads on collars and then we looked at each other
and shouted 'RUN!' and we ran outside the park
and slammed the gate on the other dogs.

Someone's excited!

How to Cope with an Abundance of Pooches

I can safely say that I have never been so exhaustified in my life.

Once we had rounded up all the dogs and returned them to their owners, even Molly had to admit that she was impressed with Frank's whistling TECHNIQUE.

I love excited!

'What did you think you were *doing* with so many dogs at once?' he asked. 'Were you trying to round up more guests for the Pooch Party, or something?'

'No, of course not!' Molly said. 'We were doing it for the cash.' She showed him the twenty pounds we had earned that day.

'Molly!' I protested. If Frank saw all that cash, he would start going on about his 'fee' again.

But he didn't. He just gave us a puzzled look.

Molly said, 'You explain, Summer.'

So I did.

'And so you see we DO need this dog-walking business to work because we really need the cash for the party, which is why we *cannot pay you* to help with the dogs,' I added with great emphasis.

'OK, I can see your problem. So forget the fee,' Frank said, smiling in a kind and totally non-evil way.

How to Cope with an Abundance of Pooches

I peered at him closely to see if he was joking. But no, he did not suddenly burst into hysterical mean laughter and point and me and say, 'Got you there, Summer! You are soooo owned!'

He simply stood there, looking back at me and waiting to see what I would say.

'Er, thank you?' I said, still waiting for him to laugh.

'You're welcome,' said Frank, grinning.

Molly was not so Gracious about Frank's kind, if slightly baffling offer. 'What are you up to, Frank Gritter?' she asked, looking at him WITHERINGLY.

'Nuffin'. I juswannidta help, thass all,' Frank muttered in his unintelligible boy-speak. I noticed he'd gone a bit pink about the ears.

'Sorry?' said Molly. 'Is my brain deceiving me by sending me false and untrue messages of a confusing nature? Did you say you wanted to help us AND you didn't want to be paid?'

Puppy Party

Frank rolled his eyes to the high heavens and then said, 'How about this for a compromise? I help you, and you invite me and Meatball to the party?'

Not even Molly could argue with that, especially as Meatball had already been on the list right from the start. But Frank didn't need to know that.

Molly had a lot to argue about once Frank was gone, however.

'I REALLY do not want him to get involved in running this party,' she fumed. 'It is All Very Well for him to help walk the dogs and come along on the day, but I do not want him sticking his big **BOGEYFIED** nose into our plans.'

I thought this was what Molly's mum would call a 'bit rich' (in other words quite cheeky) coming from Molly as Frank had totally got us out of a tight spot of trouble AND it was not even

her actual party, but I thought I should just agree
for the sake of a bit of peace and quiet so I said,
'Yes,' with a heavy sigh. 'It is rather annoying that
we have to RESORT to asking him to help, but
I think it is the only Option Two that we have
available to us. Unless you have another Option
Two about how we can raise enough money that
does not involve walking hundreds of dogs on our
own?' I added, sort of hopefully, but sort of not,
as it was quite obvious to me that Frank would
actually be a very good Addition to our plan.

Molly grimaced and said with Great
Reluctance, 'I do not have another Option Two,
or even an Option Three.'

So that was that. Frank came and helped us
to walk the dogs and we did not have any further
Major Disaster Moments. Molly made him agree
in writing that he would not ask for any money
from us. And although he rolled his eyes when he
signed her special contract, he said it was OK as

long as he could eat as many crisps and cakes as he
wanted at the party.

That goes for us too!

I, the person who has their
name on this paper, ie. Frank
Gritter, do solemnly agree not
to ask for cash or any kind
of payment at all in return
for helping Molly Cook and
Summer Love with the dog
walking. ~~And I promise not
to be a showy off know-it-
all boy either~~
                    ↖ Shut up Molly!

Frank Gritter

11
How to Reluctantly Agree to Something

By the time we had walked all the dogs in the neighbourhood that there were to walk, there were only FOUR DAYS left until the party! I was getting rather over-panical about it, as we had done literally Zero the Hero about decorations or a cake or planning games or buying the snacks or anything.

And Nick had called Mum and told her he had FORTY-FIVE people coming to the party. Mum had gone a bit white when he had said this, as our house is not very big, but Nick had told her it was too difficult not to invite them all.

'This has turned into a mega party. We are

going to have to stop doing our dog walking and start doing some party organizing,' I told Molly.

'But we've only earned fifty pounds!' Molly cried, as she counted out the last coin.

'Yay!' I cried. 'That means we have one hundred pounds in total! That is a huge and totally massive amount of money: we can probably buy even more stuff than we had thought of originally!'

I clasped my hands together in utter GLEE and grinned at my Bestest Friend.

But my Bestest Friend did not join in my gleefulness. In fact, she was strangely silent.

'Hey, Molly?' I said. 'An extra fifty pounds *is* great – isn't it?' My heart had started to flutter OMINOUSLY, in other words in a manner that was full of dread and foreboding.

Molly sighed loudly and shook her head.

I held my breath in horror.

'It's not enough,' Molly said quietly. 'When

How to Reluctantly Agree to Something

I did the hack, the whole list of stuff came to at least one hundred and fifty, and that was without a cake for April and without food for the extra guests Nick has invited.'

'WHAT?' I exclaimed. 'Why didn't you tell me?' I let my head sink into my hands. 'I'm going to call Nick,' I said in a muffled way. 'He will have to uninvite people.'

Molly reached over and put a hand on my arm. 'It's not the people, really. It's the dog treats,' she said gently. 'They are all just so expensive.'

She chewed her bottom lip thoughtfully. Then her eyes did the shiny thing they do when her brain starts to WHIRR, and her eyebrows started to rise up into her fringe, and a huge grin spread over her face.

'Of course!' she cried, slapping her leg in a dramatical fashion. 'I am so stupid.'

I was gobbersmacked and flabberboozled. I had never heard Molly call herself that before.

Puppy Party

'Dogs eat anything, don't they? You have seen what they are like in the park, eating all manner of disgusting rubbish. So we don't have to spend so much on them.'

'But I don't want my dog eating disgusting rubbish!' I protested.

Molly put her head on one side and smiled. 'I know, I don't mean *real* rubbish. What I mean is, they can eat what we eat! Like sausage rolls and mini scotch eggs and mini pizzas and crisps – it's all savoury stuff, isn't it? They will LOVE it! Yes, that's it. I will ADJUST our list, in other words change it, so that we just get a few more bits and pieces of the human-type food. And then I'll ask Mum to take us to the supermarket to get everything, OK?'

'OK,' I said. I was not one hundred and ten per cent certain that Molly really had come up with a proper solution. But what else could we do?

★

How to Reluctantly Agree to Something

Mrs Cook said that she would be happy to take
us to the supermarket the next day. It was really
kind of her to agree to take us because Mum was
at work and I would have had to catch the bus
otherwise, which would not have been easy with
a ton of shopping bags. But the bad thing about
Molly's mum taking us was that we had to wait
until she had tidied up her house first (which is
her major Number One Hobby in life) and that
apparently took ALL MORNING!

And oh my goodness dearie me did
that morning drag *on and
on and on* while I waited
for them. I must have
looked at the clock at
least fifty million times
between breakfast and
ten o'clock. I even tried
catching it by surprise a
few times by creeping

163

up on it backwards and whirling round to see if
the hands had moved on any faster, as I was sure
it was slowing down on purpose to annoy me.

It was made all the worse because I was on
my own. I suppose that's what the expression 'too
much time on your hands' means, as if I had not
been on my own, the time would have had to
spread itself around between more people. But
as it was, Mum had had to go to work, April
obviously was not there, and Honey was quite
sleepy and pooped from all the extra exercise she
had been getting with the other dogs we had been
walking, and was sleeping it off in her basket.

It's a relief to have
a morning off. *yawn*

In a fit of the Most Ultra-Boring Boredom in
Boringsville, I decided to get out Mum's laptop
and do some Surfing of the Internet. I thought

How to Reluctantly Agree to Something

I might find out some fun and interesting facts
about dogs that I did not already know and
possibly at the same time get some ideas for games
that were not as bonkers as 'musical pups' (bah!)

I decided, for a laugh, to type in 'parties for
dogs' and then looked down a long list of things,
most of which, as usual, were no use at all and
not in the slightest tiny amount interesting. But
then a site caught my eye. It was called:

HOW TO THROW A POOCH PARTY

'This looks good!' I thought, and read on:

Here are some quick tips for you to follow:

Spend a Penny!

Make sure your pup has done his/her
'business' before the event. This helps to avoid
embarrassing 'party pooper' problems!

Puppy Party

Well THAT was kind of obvious!

> ### Don't Invite Party Bores
> If a dog finds it hard to get along with unfamiliar dogs and people, it could cause havoc and will not enjoy itself either.

Of course I was only inviting the pooches I knew and cared most about in the whole entire world . . .

> ### Mood Music
> If you play music, make sure the volume is turned down so that it is soft enough for sensitive canine ears.

Oh dear, another thing to plan.

> ### Party Games
> How about a contest for things such as 'largest tail,' 'best trick' or 'floppiest ears,' with

How to Reluctantly Agree to Something

prizes or paper awards going to the winners.
For a real treat, why not hire a pet massage
therapist? Dogs receive their massage on a soft,
warm blanket!

Who on earth could get their pooch to lie still
enough to give them a massage on a blanket! I
knew Honey would not and the younger dogs
would be far too excitable. But the 'largest tail'
and 'best trick' contests sounded quite fun. The
human guests might think it was a laugh too
which would be a way of getting them to join in.

I was just starting to feel happier about the
party and more in control of things, when I read
this next bit:

Party Food

DOGS SHOULD NOT EAT THE SAME FOOD
AS YOUR HUMAN GUESTS! All dogs should
still follow their normal diets. Human food can

be very dangerous to dogs, particularly some takeaway or party food, so check out the list below to make sure you do not serve anything that will harm the dogs. You do not want to be dealing with a sick dog during your party!

I was totally and utterly flabbergasted and glued to the screen. This was an utter disaster! It was in fact mightily ՐREACHEROUS!

I closed my eyes tight and forced myself to breathe in and out as normally as possible. Then I started talking to myself to calm myself down: 'The party is really for April First and Foremost, in other words April is the most important person in this whole thing, not the pooches. If necessary we can shut them outside away from the human food and they can just play and run around until they are exhaustified.'

But I knew this was not going to work: our garden was not big enough for so many dogs to be left unsupervised. And what about it being Honey's birthday too? The whole point had been to have the party for her as well. I couldn't cancel the doggy guests because I had promised that Titch and Meatball could come. And Custard had to be there because he was the Decoy.

I made myself read through a list at the bottom of the screen of all the dangerous foods. All the things Molly had talked about – the sausage rolls, the pizza and so on and so on were on there. (And chocolate was actually a POISONOUS food for dogs – at least we had not planned on giving them any of that.)

'Oh Honey!' I said, running into the utility room, where she was snuggled up in her basket, totally Oblivious to the whole PALAVER. 'Thank goodness to mercy and all the highest heavens that I read all that important information on the Internet before it was too late!' I threw my arms around her and hugged and squeezed her.

Don't know what I've done to deserve this, But you just carry on!

I had to talk Molly straight away.

I picked up the phone there and then and Paced Up and Down the hall with Honey following at my heels and almost in fact tripping me up, while I waited what I was sure was an entire Eternity for Molly to answer.

'Hello. Molly Cook speaking,' she finally said, in her poshest telephone answering voice.

'Hello, it's me.'

'Ooooh it's yooooou! Oh, my goodness dearie me!' squealed Molly. I could literally hear her jumping up and down with excitement. 'Only a couple more hours till our shopping trip, which is going to be the totally bestest shopping trip ever! And then only THREE DAYS until the ACTUAL PARTY—!'

How to Reluctantly Agree to Something

'Yes, that's why I'm ringing,' I butted in.
Goodness I was very grateful indeed that we
were not yet at that point in the future where
everyone in the world had those phones where
you can see the person you are speaking to
and Vice Versa (in other words, the other way
around). If Molly had been able to see me while
I was talking, she would have known that I was
in a FEARSOME STATE.

Molly said, 'Oh?' as if she was not one
tiddly iota of a bit interested in what I had to
say, but because I know her so well, I could tell
that actually she was extremely vastly interested
indeed.

'It's about the dogs,' I said. And then I left
a dramatical pause, which I have to say was very
clever of me. It is something I have learned
from watching those Cliff Hanger Suspension
programmes on the telly where a character tells
a person only half a piece of information so that

they are literally hanging, as if from a cliff by the edges of their fingernails, on the every breath of what the character is saying. It is called Reeling Someone In, in other words, it means you have that person sort of in your power for a moment.

'What about the dogs?' said Molly, in an impatient, yet interested, tone.

'It's so important that I think you should come round to my place right away before we go on the actual shopping trip so that I can show you all sorts of mega-cool things I have found out on the Internet,' I said, which was kind of lying, but only slightly.

'All right, I will see if Mum will let me,' she said. I could tell that she was quite inquisitive now.

Luckily Molly did come round, *almost* straight away. She cannot resist anything about dogs, especially now that she has her own gorgeous pupsicle, Mr Titch.

That's my Boy!

'So,' she said, before I had even completely opened the front door. 'What is this extremely important piece of information about dogs on the Internet that you couldn't tell me about over the phone?'

'Come in,' I said, fixing a beamy grin on my face.

Molly followed me into the sitting room where I had the laptop ready. I had scrolled to the list of dangerous foods and I gestured to Molly to sit in front of it.

'I am so sorry about this, Molly, but I am in a total panic about the party food situation. I have found this information and I thought you should see it because you have not been an actual dog-owner-type person for really that long, and you might not know that there are foods that human people can eat that our doggie friends simply can't as otherwise they might get ill or even actually die!' I had to stop there, as I was running out of *breath* and feeling a little light in the head.

'Oh my goodness!' cried Molly, looking down the list. 'I knew about the chocolate, OBVIOUSLY – every dog-owner knows that, for goodness sake who would give their dog chocolate?' I was pretty sure she had no INKLING at all about that, but Now Was Not the Time to argue, 'But I had no *idea* about the other things!' She scanned the list rather panickedly and began wildly scrolling down the page and reading more and more. She squeaked every time she read something new, and her face got whiter and whiter. I began to feel rather ashamed that I had got her into such a state.

Eventually Molly sat back, slumped in the

How to Reluctantly Agree to Something

chair and looking like a person who has been made to run fifty times round the sports field and then been told that they will have to do it again in five minutes. Except that she actually looked worse than that, because she not only looked exhaustified and Deflated, but she had also gone very quiet and was staring at the screen as if she was in a trance.

My heart slid in a slippery fashion into my shoes as I realized we would definitely have to cancel the dog part of the party. It was all just too difficult.

Oh, no party?
sigh

I gulped. 'Are you OK, Molly?' I asked softly.

'Mmm,' she said distractivatedly. She was still staring at the screen but she was now scrolling down and reading more and more of the scary information.

'Molly,' I said, worriedly. 'You don't need to read any more. You will only make yourself more and more anxious.'

'Mmm,' said Molly. She was still reading.

'So do you think we should maybe think about cancelling the pooch bit of the party?' I muttered. Molly turned to me as I said this, and I cringed, waiting for an explosion from my Best Friend.

But there was no explosion. In fact, Molly was happily smiling at me. She also had a rather UNSETTLING look in her eyes. In other words, her eyes were glinting in a suspicious and worrying manner. In fact, it looked as though she was about to say that she had thought of a Masterly Plan.

I opened my mouth to say something, but Molly got there first. 'I've just had the most Masterly of Masterly Plans,' she said, her beaming smile turning into the sort of smile a mad-genius-

How to Reluctantly Agree to Something

inventor-type person smiles
before saying that he or she
has just discovered the secrets
of the universe, and that now
they have told you that, they
are going to have to kill you.

'Yes?' I said, trying not to
show how nervously miserable
I was feeling at the PROSPECT.

'Yes!' said Molly. 'We do not need to cancel
anything.'

'No?'

'NO! We will get some ingredients from the
supermarket this afternoon and we will *cook our
own dog food*! Look,' she said, pointing to Mum's
laptop. 'Look what it says right here: "Why not
have a go at cooking your own dog food?" And
there's a whole load of recipe links here. It is utter
geniusness.'

I was not finding Molly's enthusiasm for this

new plan very infectious. In fact, I could not help feeling that it was not an idea that was going to turn out at all well.

I have to say, I'm with Molly on this one!

12
How to Get
Carried Away

'**I**f we make our own doggy treats, this will truly be a party to remember!' Molly announced.

'But why in the high heavens above would anyone who is at all sane and normal want to COOK THEIR OWN DOG FOOD?' I asked. Molly shot me a particularly strange look.

'What?' I said.

'Er, I seem to remember that *someone* was quite keen on cooking for their pooch when that pooch was expecting *puppies*?' she said pointfully.

'No – what? Oh . . . !' I said, and suddenly I felt very silly and sheepish indeed. Because the thing is, when Honey was expecting, her eating habits went just a little bit DOOLALLY CRAZY, to say the least, and I was so worried that she was not eating properly that I looked it all up in my book, *Perfect Puppies*, and I discovered that a pregnant dog can often go off her normal food and that it can be a good idea to tempt her with other things. Such as peanut butter on toast, and scrambled egg made with butter and cream.

It Was delicious!

'That was different,' I muttered defensively. 'Honey was pregnant, and it is well known that pooches can go off their usual food at such a delicate and sometimes difficult time.'

 I Was feeling quite delicate, it's true.

How to Get Carried Away

'Anyway,' said Molly, 'I actually think it is a faberoony idea to cook for the pooches. It will be such fun! Not to mention very responsible in a dog-owner-type way, as then we can be one hundred and ten per cent certain that we will not be feeding them with ultra-dangerous and in fact positively TOXIC (i.e. poisonous) stuff. I bet you already have a lot of what we need in the cupboards, so we might not even have to spend as much from the budget as if we went out and got all those expensive doggy treats from the pet shop. In fact, let's go through the cupboards now and check off what else we need to make those recipes. We will have to re-do the shopping list, but that is OK, as I have my notebook with me anyway, so it is no Big Deal to make a few AMENDMENTS.'

I had been about to agree enthusiastically when I realized what it was Molly was IMPLYING. 'Hang on a minute,' I said slowly.

'Did you just say that *I* would already have
what we needed? As in "Let's do the cooking at
Summer's house"?'

'Ye-es,' said Molly in a tone which suggested
that I was rather stupid and Slow on the Uptake,
in other words, not on the same length of wave as
she was. 'You don't think we can do the cooking
at *my* place, do you? For a start Mum would go
bonkers doolally round the twist if she caught us
mucking up her PRISTINE kitchen, and for a
finish, it's *your* sister's party, so obviously it makes
perfect sense to be doing the cooking *here*.'

'But what if MY mum goes bonkers doolally
round the twist?' I asked. 'She wasn't exactly
chuffed to bits when she caught me cooking
scrambled eggs with butter and cream. She said,
"I've heard of cravings, but this is ridiculous," and,
"Not even I was that expensive to feed when I
was expecting," and other things of an outraged
and rather angry nature. And I can hardly even

have the good excuse of Honey being pregnant this time. PLUS if Mum finds we are cooking dog food, she will then find out the dogs are coming to the party and she will definitely then try to Put a Stop to It.'

Now why would she want to do that?

'Summer,' Molly said, in a patient-but-really-impatient tone of speaking. 'Your mum was cross last time because you used very expensive ingredients and you finished all the eggs in the house and did not replace them; whereas we have saved some of our budget for the dogs, remember? So we can always get more ingredients on our shopping trip this afternoon. And your mum is out at work today and actually quite a lot of the time, whereas mine is not, so we can cook while your mum is not here and she will not notice if we tidy up. Plus your mum is not as fussy about the pristine-ness of her kitchen as my mum is.'

'Humpf,' I said. I couldn't think of anything else to say, because as usual Molly was one hundred and ten per cent right about everything. I did not quite like what she was INSINUATING about Mum not being as fussy. It sounded as though she was hinting that my mum was not as clean and tidy as hers. But then, on second thoughts, Molly's mum was the kind of mum who does not like you to sit on the sofa for at least two days after she has cleaned it in case you make a dent in the

poofed-up cushions. Maybe it was better to have a slightly more chaotic and untidy mum after all.

We can chill out at our place.

'Well,' I said eventually. 'I suppose you are right. It is my sister's party, and it was my amazing idea to have the pooches come along too, so it is only fair that I get to organize the cooking at my house.'

Aha! I thought that was a rather clever way of me IMPOSING a bit of control on the situation. I made a mental note to try and remember such intelligent and crafty TACTICS in the future.

Molly did look ever so slightly dumbfounded and bamboozled. But I could tell that she was just really desperate to start the cooking, and she knew she could not do it at her house, so she did not argue about who had had what amazing idea. Instead she said, 'That's settled then. So, let's look at those recipes.'

We took the laptop into the kitchen and put it on the table, and Molly said she would read out

Puppy Party

the ingredients while I climbed up on to the work surface so that I could get to Eye Level with the cupboards.

'Let's start with the doggy hamburgers,' Molly suggested. 'They look like they'd be really easy to make.'

'OK,' I said, looking down. 'What do we need?'

Molly peered at the computer screen. 'Vegetable oil,' she read out.

I pushed the bottles and packages around until I caught sight of a yellowish plastic bottle. 'Check!' I said.

Molly reached for her notebook and wrote 'vegetable oil' in it and then put a big tick beside it.

'Molly,' I said. 'Why are you writing it down and then ticking it off? It is obvious we already have it, so there is no need to go to all that palaver.'

Molly pursed her lips and shook her head at

me. 'It is important to know we have all Bases Covered,' she said. 'We don't want to go all the way to the supermarket and then come back and find we should have got something ESSENTIAL, in other words something we absolutely cannot do without.'

I raised my eyes to the high heavens.

'OK,' I said. 'What next?'

'Boiled eggs,' she said. 'Two.'

I put my hands on my hips. 'Well obviously we do not keep a cupboard load of boiled eggs!' I cried. 'What nonsense.'

Molly tutted. 'You are being loonitistical,' she said. 'You just need two fresh eggs and then you boil them, you numpty!'

'Oh,' I said. 'Well Mum keeps eggs in the fridge, so why don't you have a look seeing as I am up here?'

Molly opened the fridge. 'Only four eggs there. We had better put eggs on the list then,

in case your mum freaks.' She looked up at me.
'Like last time,' she added, sniggering a bit.

'Molly, shut the door properly,' I snapped.
'Honey is ultra-talented at getting in there
otherwise.' I shuddered as I remembered the
CARNAGE, in other words mega-disastrous
mess, she had made the last time she had managed
to break and enter the fridge.

Molly went back to reading out from the
recipe and I went back to rummaging, and we
ended up with a list that looked like this:

1 packet beef mince
Box of eggs
Handful green beans
2 carrots
Packet of cottage cheese

YUM!

How to Get Carried Away

The only other things we needed were porridge oats and the vegetable oil, both of which Mum had in the cupboards. No one in our family has ever actually eaten porridge, thankfully. In fact, it was only there because April used it to make her own gunky face pack which was a horrid grey *gloopy* mixture she used to leave in the fridge and which smelt terrible.

Mum will probably be only too glad to have the oats used up instead of leaving them to clutter up the cupboard, I told myself.

But in actual fact I could not get rid of the sinking feeling that Mum was not going to be very glad about any of the details of this latest Molly Cook-style Masterful Plan.

13

How to Make a Dog's Breakfast of Everything

When we got back from the supermarket, it was already getting late. Mum was due back from work at six, so we had to crack on with the cooking right away.

'It says we need to fry the mince first,' Molly said.

'Easy!' I said cheerily. I had done that before when Mum let me help make Bolognese. I poured a small dollop of vegetable oil into a frying pan, carefully tipped the meat in and then stirred it with a wooden spoon.

'Right, now we need to let it cool so we can mix it with the other stuff,' I said. 'Hang on, we need to boil the eggs. You do that, Molly, while I get those beans and carrots out and see what the recipe says to do with them.'

The recipe said the veg had to be chopped up 'finely'. I did not know what 'chopping veg finely' meant. I thought it might mean that you had to do it like a *posh* chef would do; you know, the kind of chef who only cooks Fine Food, but seeing as I was not that sort of a cook and could only really manage things like toast and scrambled eggs on my own without Mum's SUPERVISION (in other words without her helping me) I did not think I could do this 'finely'. Molly was busy timing the eggs as apparently it was important to make sure they boiled for the exact amount of time that was correct for boiling eggs. I did not want to distractivate her, so instead of worrying about how to chop the veg, I decided to put the beans and carrots in the one saucepan to save washing up, and then get out the hand-whizzer-food-processory thing that I had seen Mum use. Using an APPLIANCE, in other words a machine, will be a super-speedy way of chopping and will be quite professionalist too, I thought.

I plugged it in, put the blade bit into the saucepan full of veg and pressed the ON button.

Unfortunately the result was not at all chef-like or professionalistic in any way. In fact, you could say that the carrots and the beans reacted very badly to the whole experience. They did a sort of a **Food Protest**. They leaped out of the saucepan and flew into the air. And some of them got stuck to the ceiling and walls.

'Waaah!' I screamed, jumping back.

'Summerwhadareyoudooooing?' Molly screamed, dropping the eggs she was trying carefully to extractivate from the saucepan. At least they were hard boiled, so the yolks could not run all over the place.

How to Make a Dog's Breakfast of Everything

'I don't know!' I shouted. 'Honey – don't—!'

Honey had Taken Advantage of the Culinary Chaos (in other words, my disastrous cooking) to help herself to a little pre-party tasting session.

Which means that she rushed over and gobbled up the eggs and any bits of veg that had fallen to the floor. Actually, she did not hoover up the veg with any particular enthusiasm.

Eggs are yum-licious.
Not that keen on those
greeny-orange bits though.

'Look at the time!' Molly gasped. 'We must hurry and clear this lot up and start again before your mum gets home and—'

'Before I get home and *what* exactly?'

Mum *had* got home. And early too, I noticed, glancing at the clock.

Molly **FROZE** in mid-actual-sentence and

Puppy Party

I went into Full-On Quivering and Quaking
Mode. In some ways we were quite lucky because
Honey had finished clearing up the eggs (although
she was not much use at dealing with the mess
that had sprayed down on to the floor and the
lower-level kitchen cupboards and the ceiling).
But in other ways, we were not lucky at all.

'SUMMER!' Mum actually bellowed. I do
not think I have seen her that angry ever. In my
entire life. Not even the time that Honey got into
the fridge and ate everything in it . . .

How to Make a Dog's Breakfast of Everything

'I – er – I'm – s-s-s-sorry,' I whispered. I looked at Molly for support, but she was shaking her head furiously at me and backing away towards the door.

Mum had done a good job of Barring the Exit, though. In other words, she was standing in the doorway, her hands on her hips, her nostrils doing their SCARY FLARY thing they do when she is beside herself, in other words, furious. She was not going to let Molly escape in a million years.

'WHAT kind of a dog's breakfast is *this*?' Mum said, in a low and dangerous tone which was actually more frightening than her bellowing voice. I was struck dumb by how she knew already that we were cooking for the dogs, even though it was not true to say it was for breakfast.

'Please, sorry, er . . . sorry,' said Molly in an un-Molly-like babbling fashion. 'We were making some food for the party.'

'Really,' Mum said, with one eyebrow very

much arched. 'Well, *I* am sorry, but I think if there is going to be any food made for this party, I think *I* will be making it. Otherwise I doubt I shall be left with a house to live in.'

I gasped and stared at Molly with my eyes boggling out of their sockets. Mum could not do that! She could not take over!

'NO!' I cried. 'I mean, you can't do that, you are too vastly busy and Run Off Your Feet with work-type things and looking after me! Molly and I will clear up this mess and start again tomorrow.'

'Well you're right about one thing,' Mum said, folding her arms in a Decisive manner. 'You can certainly clear this lot up. Right now. But after that, you and Molly can be in charge of decorations, and *I* will be in charge of everything else.'

Do I still get to slurp food off the floor?

How to Make a Dog's Breakfast of Everything

This was a total and utter Disaster Area. On a scale of one to a hundred of possible disasters, we had hit about two thousand.

'I think we will have to talk to Nick,' I told Molly once we had cleaned up and cleared off. 'Custard was going to be our Decoy for getting April to the party in the first place, and now if we are not going to have pooches there at all, how is that going to work?'

'Oooh no,' said Molly, shaking her head. 'There is no way we are giving up on the pooch party idea.'

'But Molly—!'

'Listen,' said my Bestest Friend, looking the most determined I have ever seen her. 'I never thought I would say this, but I am hatching a Masterly Plan which involves someone who I would not usually in a million trillion gazillion light years even CONSIDER asking to help us, but as you know, Desperate Times Call For Desperate Measures, and this is about as desperate as we are ever likely to be . . .' She paused for dramatical effect and then said with a big sigh: 'Frank Gritter.'

'What about him?' I asked.

'Frank Gritter,' Molly repeated. 'Though I do actually DETEST having to admit it, he was a huge help with the dog walking, and he does want to come to the party.'

I was utterly flabberboozled by this bonkers suggestion. Frank could be a good laugh and it Could Not Be Denied that he knew a lot about dogs, but . . .

'BUT . . . ASK FRANK TO COOK??!!' I shouted. 'Are you INSANE?'

'Possibly,' said Molly. 'But I am also desperate. Aren't you?'

What could I say to that?

I had expected Frank to laugh in our faces and say something along the lines of the fact that he would prefer to dress in a tutu and pirouette

How to Make a Dog's Breakfast of Everything

across the football pitch in
front of all his mates rather
than help a couple of GIRLS
do some cooking for a party.
But, as has happened a
few times in the past,
now I come to think of
it, Frank did in fact totally
surprise me and COME Up
TRUMpS, in other words he
was utterly marvellous.

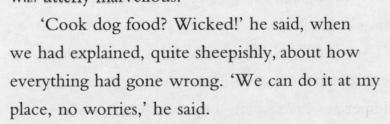

'Cook dog food? Wicked!' he said, when
we had explained, quite sheepishly, about how
everything had gone wrong. 'We can do it at my
place, no worries,' he said.

'But, er, won't your mum mind?' I asked. 'I
mean, it might be a bit messy.'

'Nah,' said Frank. 'I love cooking. Mum lets
me cook a load of stuff in the holidays when I'm
a bit bored or whatever.'

Puppy Party

'A right little Masterchef,' said Molly, but very very under her breath. She knew that Frank was our Only Hope, after all.

'Bring the ingredients round this afternoon and we'll sort it. And you can keep the food at mine until the party, so no one needs to find out,' he added, giving me one of his huge and intensively annoying winks. I replied by giving him a smile that was more like a cringe-some wince and said, 'Thank you, Frank.'

We walked most of the way back to our houses in silence.

As I said goodbye to Molly, I said, 'I think I will be glad when this party is over.'

'Yes,' she agreed. Then she said, 'Well at least everything is now more or less sorted. All we have to do now is decorate the house, lay the tables with the food on the day and wait for the guests to arrive. Surely nothing else could possibly go wrong?'

14

How to Have a Hysterical Nervous Breakdown

As I walked round the corner to my own house, I felt relaxed for the first time in days. In other words I finally could no longer feel a room full of butterflies fluttering around inside my tummy and I did not feel sick and nervous and anxious at the thought of the party. In fact I actually skipped along the pavement and was singing to myself by the time I got to our driveway.

'Hello!' I shouted, as I let myself in. 'Anybody hom—'

A strange noise interrupted me in mid-flow of shouting. 'Waaaah!'

Cheese and Toast came hurtling down the hall,

ears flat, and fur all spiked up, howling as if someone had set fire to their tails. Honey was in Hot Pursuit, but when she saw me she skidded to a halt and wrapped herself round my legs, whining and whimpering. I was more than a tiny bit freaked out.

'Waaaaah!' There was that awful shrieking again.

What in all the earth was going on?

'Mum?' I asked, in a hesitatingly and questioning type of way. It did not actually sound a bit like Mum, but who else could it be . . . ? I thought about following the example of Cheese and Toast and scarpering back outside but then I heard: 'Booo hoooo! He's at it agaaaaaaain!'

Oh. My. Goodness. Dearie. Me. It was April.

whimper It's a scary noise that girl is making.

Thank goodness I had not barged in and shouted out stuff about the party, I thought. Then I realized that that was probably the least of my worries, as April's crying had gone Up A Notch, in other words it was in the realm of wailing now.

My ears are hurting!

'I read his texts!' she said, looking up as I came through the door.

April was sitting at the kitchen table, a mammoth mound of wet and crumpled tissues next to her. Her head was in her hands, her normally shiny and ultra-groomed hair was messier than the messiest bird's nest (which is probably a bit unfair to birds, but you get the picture) and her make-up was smeared in an alarmingly clownish fashion all over her face. This did not bode well. She looked like the Creature from the Swampy Lagoon.

'April?' I said quietly. I hovered near the door in case I needed to make a quick getaway. When April was like this she was Mad, Bad and Dangerous to know. In fact, even when she wasn't like this she was Mad, Bad and Dangerous to know, but the Swampy Lagoon look meant she was likely to be even Madder and Badder.

'How could he *do* this to me? We haven't been married a *year* yet!' she continued.

'Is Mum here?' I asked, still making sure I was keeping a Safe Distance. I noticed poor Honey was COWERING under the table. I wished I could actually join her down there instead of in this dangerous war zone of sobbing and wailing and nose-blowing.

April chewed at one of her ultra-long and perfectly manicured nails and bit it right off. Gross.

How to Have a Hysterical Nervous Breakdown

And a waste of time given the amount of hours she DEVOTED to filing and painting them. But I didn't say that out loud. I was quite frightened of the Wild Look on my sister's face. As well as the black mascara tears running down her cheeks, she had an insane and crazy sparkle in her eyes as if she was plotting something unpleasant.

'He'd better watch out when he comes home tonight!' she hissed, picking up a mobile phone from under the yucky mound of tissues. Oh dear, she WAS plotting something unpleasant.

It's safer down here, Believe me.

'April,' I said, quietly and soothingly in the way that people do on the telly when they are talking to DANGEROUS CRIMINAL TYPES with a gun or to a particularly wild animal. 'April, put the phone down and listen to me.' I took one slow step nearer the hissing spitting creature before me.

April did a weird snarl and actually bared her teeth at me. I decided she must be having some kind of Hysterical Nervous Breakdown. I jumped out of the way and decided to Hold My Position by the door in case something truly unpredictable happened.

'Why don't you give me the phone and I'll make us a nice cup of tea,' I said. I was eyeing the kettle, thinking that I could just about edge my way round the room to it without her being able to lash out and hit me in any way, as long as I squished myself up against the cupboards.

She gave a half-snarl that was not as scary as

the one before and then her face crumpled and
more black swampy tears fell gloopily down her
pink cheeks and she sobbed, 'That would be ni-i-
ice.' She ended with a hiccup, and that was when
I stopped feeling scared and started feeling sorry
for her. She was, after all, my Big Sis whom I
had actually come to rather miss having around
the place, and she obviously was really upset. I
stopped thinking at that point and just Acted on
my Instincts, in other words I rushed up to her
and gave her a hug.

Now we are not sisters who Do Hugs most
of the time. In fact if someone had come into
the house there and then and asked me, 'Summer
Holly Love, when is the last time you gave your
Big Sis an actual hug?' I would first of all have
asked them what they thought they were doing
barging in on us when we were having such an
Emotional Scene, and then I would have said,
'Er, I don't rightly remember.' Or words to that

effect, as I don't really ever say 'rightly' like that, now I come to think of it.

But, as Molly says: Desperate Times Call for Desperate Measures, in other words, sometimes it is only a hug that will do in certain situations.

April gripped me tightly and wailed even harder than ever.

I counted to ten, which allowed what I thought was an acceptable amount of time to let my sis DRENCH my clothing with her CoₚloUS AND ABUNDANꞇ tears of a salty and extremely moist nature, and then I PRISED myself away. In other words, I gently pushed *her* away from *me*. And then I said, 'I'll get that cup of tea, then.'

I almost tiptoed to the kettle and held my breath as I waited for April to wail again. But she didn't. She picked up the phone again and waved it at me and said, 'Just listen to this, OK?' and then she looked at the phone and read out loud:

How to Have a Hysterical Nervous Breakdown

'And they *all* have kisses after them! And they are all from WITHHELD NUMBERS!!' April was positively screechifying now, and was waving the phone so violently I pressed myself as far back as I could against the work surface without actually jumping on top of it.

Oh Boy, she's off again.

Puppy Party

'I – I don't think you've got anything to worry about,' I said, ever so slightly lamely, 'I expect Nick is just planning something he doesn't want you to know – oh!' I gasped and my hands flew to my face as all of a sudden everything came into focus in my brain. It was like I was doing a very complicated jigsaw puzzle and all at once I had found the pieces that had been missing and I knew where to put them.

THE PARTY!! How in all the earth could I have forgotten? I was a totally loop-the-loop bonkers doolally fruit-loop of a certifiably insane nature!

Nick had been sending *secret texts to invite people*, and he had been very clever and had removed their names from his address book so that April would not be able to find out what he was doing, as April was NOTORIOUSLY nosy (in other words, everyone knew how good she was at finding things out).

How to Have a Hysterical Nervous Breakdown

Except, poor Nick, his plan had not worked.

'Hold on a minute,' I said, feeling puzzled. 'How did you get hold of Nick's phone? Surely he needs it for work and stuff?'

'No, YOU hold on a minute,' said April, talking over me. 'Why did you just gasp like that? You know what he's up to, don't you?'

Don't tell
her anything!

April was snarling again and I had started to shake. 'N–n–no,' I stammered. 'I mean y–y–yes. I mean n–n–no.' That wasn't going to get me anywhere at all. I decided to try and sound AUTHORITATIVE, in other words in control (which by the way was not how I was feeling even one tiny fragment of a bit), and I repeated my question, 'How did you get hold of Nick's phone?'

Puppy Party

April actually growled. I let out a small scream.

Not you too!

'Firstly,' she said menacingly, and held up one
chewed finger, 'I got hold of Nick's phone
because I am his WIFE and I am ALLOWED to.
Secondly,' she held up another finger, 'I was going
to drop it into the surgery because I thought he
might need it, and thirdly,' another finger went up
in the air, 'the phone beeped while I was on the
way there and that's how I know about the texts.
It wasn't like I was snooping or anything. They
just appeared on the screen.'

'Whatever you say!' I said nervously. I
concentrated on pouring the boiling water from
the kettle and rummaging for a nice biscuit to
help calm April down.

She continued to rant and rave. 'He tells me
that I'm jealous and that it's silly because there

How to Have a Hysterical Nervous Breakdown

is nothing to be jealous about, and he tells me
that it's all in my mind when I see him with that
HORRENDOUS nurse, what was her name?
Felicity Big Bum, or something equally stupid,
and then he gets me under false pretences to
marry him and then we've only been married a
few months and it's nearly my BIRTHDAY for
goodness sake and already he's planning secret
trysts with half the women in the neighbourhood
by the looks of it. In fact I wouldn't be surprised
if he'd got back together with Miss Huge
Backside and that she was trying to keep me
guessing by using more than one mobile to
contact him. That is the kind of undercover
subterfuge horrible old bats like that use to try and
steal other people's husbands . . .'

I let her shout and tear at her hair while I
tried desperately to make my brain go into some
kind of useful gear to help me find a way out of
this. Poor Nick. He was soooo not the kind of

guy to get involved in those 'tryst' things April was going on about.

Eventually April ran out of steam and breath and everything else, and flopped her head on to her hands on the tabletop and cried quietly to herself.

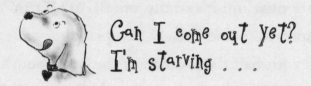

Can I come out yet? I'm starving . . .

I gently put the cup of tea down in front of her and said, 'Would you like me to talk to him?'

I thought, 'At least that way I can prevent her from rushing to the surgery with her make-up round her ankles and her hair sticking up like a **STARK RAVING PORCUPINE**, and she won't go and say anything she will regret.'

April raised her head slowly and looked at me in a bemused sort of fashion. 'You?' she said, as if I was a magical fantastical creature who did not in real life actually exist.

'Mmm,' I said, nodding. My heart was sort of banging against my ribs as I waited for her to start ranting again.

But instead of ranting, April suddenly looked severely exhaustified. 'OK,' she said. 'But I'm staying right here with this phone in case the Big Bottomed One phones.'

'Er, I think I should take the phone as evidence,' I said, thinking On My Feet, which does not mean that my brain had relocated itself to my general sock area, but that I had a quick and sudden clever thought. I paused, thinking, I will never get away with this, but April just silently handed me the phone, and before she could change her mind or try to follow me, I whizzed to the door, grabbed my jacket and was gone.

Wait for me! Got to get outta this madhouse . . .

15
How to Ruin
a Surprise

I didn't bother trying to be polite to Nasal
Penelope at the surgery.

'I need to see Nick,' I said, standing as tall as I
could, which was only to the edge of the counter,
but it would have to do. 'It's an emergency.
It's about his wife – who also happens to be my
sister,' I added, for Good Measure.

'I – well,' said Nasal Woman. I was pleased
to see that she looked suitably alarmed. She also
couldn't think of anything much to say to my
announcement (especially since I had Honey with
me this time, so I could be an actual Bona Fide
patient, in other words I might really need to

see a vet). So she backed uneasily away from the
reception desk and tapped on the door behind her,
while keeping one eye very firmly fixed on me.

She called to Nick, who came rushing out,
looking very flustered indeed. He had a syringe in
one hand, I noticed. It made me gulp looking at it.
I do not have a very Good History with syringes . . .

Neither do I.

Nick saw me looking at the syringe and hastily
put it down on the desk in front of him. 'What is
it, Summer?' he asked. 'Oh, you've got Honey.
What's up, girl?' he asked my pooch.

 You have no idea of
the day I've had.

'Can I talk to you in private?' I asked, flicking my
eyes sideways at Nasal Penelope.

'Sure,' Nick said, also flicking his eyes in her direction. Phew, thank the high heavens that April had at least married a sensible man who could read coded messages and was not like other grown-ups who needed things spelled out for them in +FOUR-FOOT-HIGH+ NEON-COLOURED +CAPITAL +LETTERS+.

Nick beckoned me and Honey to follow him, saying over his shoulder to Nasal Penelope: 'Give me a few minutes before sending in the next patient, won't you please? I'll give you a shout when I'm ready.'

'Give me a *shout*?' I heard her mutter as I followed Nick into his Consulting Room. 'Yes sir, no sir, three bags full, sir.'

I did wonder why she had chosen that moment in time to start whispering childish nursery rhymes under her breath, but then I thought, well she is a weirdo, so anything is possible. And anyway, I had more important things to be thinking about at that exact moment.

How to Ruin a Surprise

I waited until Nick had closed the Consulting Room door and then I realized I had forgotten to plan a conversation in my head. So I just panicked and blurted out: 'April thinks that you don't love her any more and that you are in true life seeing someone else.'

And I think that shrieking girl should see a vet.

Nick's face went from puzzled through to completely drained of its normal healthy pinkish colour to a rather worrying greenish shade, and he gripped the side of his vet's table hard as though he might fall over if it wasn't there to steady him.

'How? What? Where?' He babbled
INCOHERENTLY, which is a posh word I
learned from Molly to describe when someone is
talking non-stop rubbish.

'I don't know how or what or where,' I said.
'But I came in today and I found her in a rage
and crying and looking as frankly terrifyingly
monster-like as the day she had that row with
you outside our house with the Bottom Shuffler—'

'I'm sorry,' Nick cut in, waving a hand to
stop me in mid-flow. 'Who exactly is the Bottom
Shuffler?'

I rolled my eyes in an over-the-top dramatical
fashion and said, 'Yoooouu knooow.'

Nick shook his head.

'The Bottom Shuffler! Your nurse. Who
thankfully does not appear to be working here
any more.'

'Ah, you mean Felicity!' he said, blushing
slightly. 'Yes, that was all a bit unfortunate. But

she's long gone. In fact, she left of her own accord when April and I got engaged. So I'm sorry, you're going to have to start all over again. I don't understand why April should think I'm seeing Felicity.'

So I took a deep breath and told him about the text messages, handing back his phone.

'Oh no!' he said, slapping his forehead.

I jumped up and put a RESTRAINING, in other words calming, hand on his arm. 'Nick! There is no need to punish yourself by getting violent!' I cried.

Has the world of humans gone insanely mad?

'Listen!' Nick said, looking a bit wild and fierce. 'I am an *idiot*! I thought that if I deleted the names of people from my phone, then it would prevent April from getting suspicious about the party if she checked my texts by accident –' as if it would be by accident! I thought. April is far too cunning for that! But I did not say that out loud – 'but of course what has happened is that April thinks I'm sending loads of *secret texts* to another woman. Or worse – *lots* of other women!'

I nodded, feeling quite a lot of bafflement, but thinking that at least Nick was thinking things through in some way or another.

'We're going to have to tell her,' said Nick. 'It's a shame, and I know you wanted it to be a surprise, but I can't have her going around believing that I'm cheating on her! She's my wife for heaven's sake.'

'But you can't *tell* her!' I protested. 'Molly and I have done so much work to keep it all a secret and we've planned so much and we've even had to ask Frank to get involved, and you know how much Molly hates to involve Frank.' I stopped. Nick was glaring at me like I have never seen him glare before.

'I'm sorry, Summer,' he said, taking off his vet's coat and grabbing his jacket and his car keys.

A man of action – I like that!

Nick turned and fixed me with a dramatical look. 'My marriage is more important than a birthday surprise,' he declared.

I supposed he was right about that.

I told Nick that I thought April would still be at ours, as she would want to talk to Mum when she got in from work, so he told me to come with him. Nasal Penelope was not best pleased at having to deal with a load of patients who had to be told to go home and come back another day, but I don't think she had ever seen Nick glare before either, so she actually quite MEEKLY, in other words calmly, did as she was told.

'I only hope your mum sees that this is all in April's head,' Nick said grimly, as he drove rather wildly in and out of the traffic, taking short cuts and speeding along frankly faster than was usually a good idea to do.

It was a bit like being in a cops and robbers show, except that no one was following us.

This is exciting!

We arrived just in time. April was leaving the house, looking Grim and Determined. Her hair was a bit smoother and she had wiped the black streaky tracks of mascara off her cheeks. Mum was standing on the doorstep, her arms crossed, shaking her head in bewilderment.

Nick screeched to a halt in the driveway, yanked on the handbrake and jumped out of the car before he had even turned the engine off. It would have been cool if it had not also been teeth-grindingly panic-making.

Mum frowned at me and mouthed, 'What are you doing?'

April screamed. 'Get away from me!'

Nick put out his hands to calm her as though she was a RAGING LION about to pounce and rip his guts out. 'Listen, April. You've got it all wrong.'

I quickly ran to Mum who, even if she had believed April's utter lunacy and was cross with Nick too, would be infinitely more likely to listen to me than April would.

I'm loving all this running and leaping about.

'She has got it all wrong, Mum,' I told her breathlessly. 'The texts – she's told you about the texts, hasn't she? – they were to people asking

them to come to the You Know What! The
P-A-R-T-Y,' I mouthed.

'OH!' Mum gasped, her hands flying to her
mouth.

She ran down the drive just in time to stop
April thumping Nick. At least, I think that's what
she had been about to do. She had one hand
raised in the air anyway. I don't think she was
putting it up to ask a question.

'STOP!' cried Mum, stepping swiftly between
Nick and my sister. April jumped back in alarm
and let her hand fall.

I breathed out in a big whoosh.

'You are making a mistake, April,' Mum said.
She put her hands on April's shoulders and looked
her firmly in the eye. 'Nick was texting people
because Summer and I have been planning a
surprise for you.'

I make a strangled squealing noise, but Mum
threw me a warning glance which was pretty

scary actually, so I made a zipping motion with my hand across my mouth and Mum nodded.

'Summer and I thought it would be nice to throw a party for you for your birthday as we have been missing you,' she said.

As Mum explained about the secret, April's face crumpled. Then she started blubbing all over again.

Here we go . . .

Honestly, you can't get anything right with my sister. Either she thinks something is going on behind her back and she is angry about it, or she finds out that you are planning a lovely party for her and she cries about *that*!

'Oh, oh, I'm sooooo sorreeeeee!' she wailed, throwing her arms around Mum and then collapsing into Nick's arms and showering him with yucksome kisses which were just too insanely hideous to be a WITNESS of. 'I love you ALL and I don't deserve you. I am sooorreeeee!'

Well, you are right about not deserving us, I thought crossly. And right now, I'm not even that sure I want to go through with this whole party thing any more at all.

I left her blubbling into Nick's arms while I paced up and down worrying about what I was now going to say to Molly. I now had to face telling her that all our hard work had been utterly In Vain. The party was no longer a surprise one, the food was now all planned by Mum, and Frank had all the fun of making the dog treats without me and Molly. We were completely Surplus to Requirements, in other words, not needed at all.

Mum saw how anxious I was looking and gently put her arm around me. She gave me a squeeze and said, 'Don't worry, Summer. We can still make this the best party ever. And there are some things April doesn't know about, aren't there?'

'What, like the fact we've bought cheesy puffs and that you have cooked loads of homemade snacks and are providing sparkly pink wine for the grown-ups? Wow, big fat hairy deal!' I said, grumpily.

That evening April and Nick stayed for tea, and they helped me and Mum put up the balloons and some streamers. Then Nick made April promise that she would make a Grand Entrance at the party the next day so that all the guests would not be disappointed, because of course they still thought it was a surprise party.

No chance of April NOT making a Grand Entrance, I thought to myself miserably. That is the only thing my sister *does* know how to do, she is such a **Dramatical Drama Queen**.

229

Puppy Party

But at the last minute, Nick came to the
rescue of my deeply dark and depressive mood.
When it was time for April and Nick to go home,
Nick took advantage of a moment when April
was saying goodbye to Mum and whispered
to me, 'I have to make this a party April will
remember if it's the last thing I do. Are you up
for it?'

'You betcha!' I said.

'OK. Call me tomorrow,' he said with a
cryptical look. 'Between us we will make sure *no
one* will forget this birthday bash.'

16
How to Surprise
Nearly Everyone

And in the end, it was a fantastical party,
I have to say. And mostly thanks
to Nick's last minute suggestions, which
thank the high heavens, Molly thought were
BRILLIANTISSIMO. And Frank was a super-
duper huge help with the food, which left Molly
and me loads of time to make all the decorations.
We put the paw-print cut-outs in the windows,
and we made long strips of bunting from pages cut
from magazines, which saved us some money and
made a very colourful display for the sitting room
and the patio area. And we bought loads more
party streamers and party poppers for people to pop

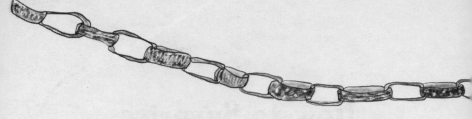

and throw at April when she arrived. The place looked festive and fab.

The guests all arrived early just as we had asked them to, and they brought mountains of exciting-looking presents wrapped in colourful posh tissue paper and that see-throughy plasticky paper that makes everything look so shiny. Mum started pouring out p*ink* *bubbly* w*ine* and lemonade and handed round the delicious nibbles Molly and I had bought with our budget and some yummy snacks she had made herself too.

I waited in the kitchen for Frank and Molly to arrive with their dogs and the food Frank had made (which at that point I still had not seen, and which Frank was being decidedly vastly secretive about, which

232

did alarm me somewhat, I have to say . . .).
They came round the back of the house and
Molly waited quietly at the bottom of the
garden with the dogs, so that Mum would not
freak out about the dogs being there. Then Frank
brought the food into the kitchen, all covered up.

DING DONG!

'Ssssh! She's here!' said Mum. The guests
huddled into the sitting room and Mum shut the
door on them and went to let Nick and April in.

'Hello, April! Hello, Nick!' Mum said, in
a far-too-loud announcementy tone. 'Oh,
you've brought Custard, how lovely.'
Then she did a massive wink and April
started to get the giggles. What
idiots we all are, I suddenly
thought. The people in the
sitting room think they are about to

surprise April, April thinks she is playing a sort of trick on them because she already knows all about it, and I am bubbling with excitement because of the dogs. We are all total loonies!

Nick opened the sitting-room door and gave April a little push into the room, then he shouted: 'SURPRISE!' and all the guests shouted, 'Surprise!' too and 'Happy Birthday!' and chucked party streamers at April and let off the party poppers, and she went all teary and hugged everyone.

I grabbed Custard by the collar and Nick by the elbow and said, 'Get April out into the garden as quickly as possible.' Then I legged it out the back to join the others.

What's going on?

Frank was sitting on the bench, but apart from him, the garden was empty.

How to Surprise Nearly Everyone

'Where's Molly? Are you ready, Molls?' I
called out.

Molly peeped out from behind the shed, her
face shiny and giggly with excitement. 'The dogs
are behind here!' she said. 'I'm keeping them
quiet with some of those homemade biscuits.
They love them!'

These are not just Biscuits, they
are Frank Gritter's Biscuits!

Custard was straining at his collar to go and join
the others, so I let him go.

Save some biscuits for me!

'I'll just grab some of the treats,' Frank said, and
whizzed into the kitchen, zooming back out again
with a plate full of his homemade dog treats.

'Nick!' I called through the door, 'Come on!'

Puppy Party

Nick and April came out, clutching their glasses and laughing, the guests following.

It was then that Frank gave one of his mega-whistles, and Honey, Titch, Meatball and Custard came bounding up to him from the bottom of the garden.

'Jump!' he shouted, and threw some special doggy burgers in the air.

All the dogs jumped to catch the food, but Honey leaped the highest and caught the whole of her burger, rather skilfully, I should say, in her mouth.

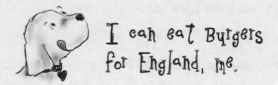

I can eat Burgers for England, me.

Then Frank said, 'Sit!' and the dogs all very obediently sat and received a mini 'canine quiche' as a reward.

'This is amazing, Summer!' Mum said.

How to Surprise Nearly Everyone

'Although I must admit, I was not prepared for all these dogs, there's not really enough room for everyone out here . . .' She raised her eyebrows at the guests who were piling out of the house into our small garden.

'But Mum,' I said. 'It's Honey's birthday too. We couldn't leave her out.'

The guests were hanging out of the open sitting-room window, peering out of the utility-room door and perched wherever they could find a space on the patio. They watched and applauded as Molly, Frank and I then did a demonstration of a mini dog-agility routine that we had secretly practised at the ELEVENTH HOUR (in other words at the last panicky moment) before the party. Nick had given me the idea when I had called him, and I must say, it was a superbly *fabulous* idea, as it was truly like as if actual Crufts had come to April's birthday party.

I have to say that little Custard stole the show

when he did a brilliant job of following the other dogs through a slalom course we had made from broom handles stuck in the grass, and jumped over buckets and rolled on to his tummy and begged for a homemade dog biscuit.

Who wouldn't look cute for a biscuit?

The dogs were pretty exhausted after that and drank huge bowls of water before collapsing in a heap on the lawn. So Molls had been right – controlling them with games and food had worked Like A Dream.

'Summer,' said April, giving me a rare sisterly hug. 'This is the best party ever. I can't believe how much trouble you've gone to.'

'It's not over yet,' said Nick.

'SURPRISE!' we shouted for the second time that day, as Nick whirled April round to

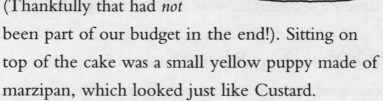

face Mum who had appeared
with a truly fanterabulacious
birthday cake make of
chocolate and creamy
layers which she had
ordered from one of the
poshest shops in town.
(Thankfully that had *not*
been part of our budget in the end!). Sitting on
top of the cake was a small yellow puppy made of
marzipan, which looked just like Custard.

Everyone burst into a round of
SPONTANEOUS singing of ♫ Happy
Birthday♪ and April cut the cake and made a
wish and went all teary again.

'It's a shame Honey doesn't have a cake,' said
April, as she handed out slices of the chocolate
one. 'Maybe she could have a slice of this?'

'NO!' chorused Molly, Nick, Frank and I.

April looked upset.

'What we mean is,' Nick said, 'there's no need, is there, Frank?'

'Eh?' I said, looking at Molly in a puzzled fashion. She pulled down the corners of her mouth as if to say, 'Don't look at me.'

Frank grinned and pushed past everyone to go back into the house. He emerged carrying a rather large something that was covered in a tea towel.

'Da-daaaaah!' he sang out in an ANNoUNCERY fashion, and flung the tea towel off to reveal what was underneath.

'Another cake?' I said.

'Yes!' said Frank. 'But this one really is for Honey!'

For little old me? Doh, you shouldn't have . . .

It was totally the most amazing thing I had ever seen — a mountainous cake made of dog food in three layers that got smaller towards the top, with those bone-shaped biscuits all around the edge of it to sort of hold it together. It looked like a fairytale castle (except that it was made of meat, which of course was pretty seriously **FREAKY** in the realm of cakes, and I doubt anyone from a fairytale would actually have appreciated it, unless they were a fairytale dog). And best of all, on the top was a flag which Frank had made from a photo of Honey, stuck to a lolly stick. It was utterly stupendously hurrah-makingly WONDERFUL.

April burst out laughing and clapped her hands, Nick said, 'Good effort, mate!'

and Mum looked rather overwhelmed and said,
'What a lovely thing to do, Frank.'

Even Molly said, 'So that's what you were up
to, Masterchef! That is absolutely brilliant!'

Lemme at it!

No, me!

I'm the smallest . . .

Hey, it's my Birthday!

As for me, I couldn't help it, I was so overcome
that Frank Gritter had made such an effort for the
birthday of my beloved pooch that I rushed over
and kissed him on the cheek!

It is not something I will now ever live down

all the days of my life, I am sure,
but there you are. Sometimes
emotions can Get the Better Of
You.

Luckily, before anyone
could comment or say,
'OoooooOOOOoooo!' in a
sneery way or ask me if Frank
was my boyfriend, Nick burst
into another Rendition of Happy
Birthday, this time for Honey,
and all the guests joined in.

Then we took the cake and gave the pooches
a chunk each as a reward for their agility show.

After that everyone just Milled Around the
place, in other words the party got a bit grown-
uppish and boring. In fact I was just thinking that
it might be a good time to ask if Molly, Frank and
I could leave and go to the park with the pooches
for a while, when April coughed loudly and tapped

the side of her glass to get everyone's attention.

'Thank you all for keeping today a surprise from me! As you no doubt know,' she said, looking at me pointedly, 'it is very difficult to keep secrets from me, as I have a habit of finding things out . . .'

Molly and Frank started sniggering uncontrollably at this point, but they quickly stopped when April glared at them too.

'But,' she went on, 'I think you have all done a brilliant job. Thank you so much, Nick, Mum, Frank – and especially Summer and Molly.'

Everyone clapped and cheered which was rather embarrassing-making, but quite cool too.

'However!' April shouted above the noise and waved her hands to get everyone to be quiet again. 'There is still one surprise left,' she said, putting her arm around Nick and looking at him in a totally loved-up soppy way. 'We have an announcement, don't we, darling?' she said to Nick, who nodded in a bashful way.

How to Surprise Nearly Everyone

The guests began murmuring excitedly among themselves. I looked quizzically at Mum, wondering if she knew what April was talking about. Mum shrugged, but she had gone weirdly pink in the face as if she was going to cry . . .

'Come on then, out with it!' someone cried.

April looked at Nick.

'You tell them,' he said. 'It's your party.'

'OK,' said April. Then she took a deep breath and announced: 'We're going to have a baby!'

'YAAAAAY!' I cried, leaping in the air and clapping my hands.

The whole party burst into hugely uproarious cheers and laughter and all the guests crowded round April, Nick and Mum to say congratulations, which made the garden into the most uncomfortable of squeezes, but was also rather lovely.

'Wow,' said Molly above all the hubbub and general chaos. 'You're going to be an auntie, Summer!'

'Cool!' said Frank. 'Can I call you that from now on: Auntie Summer?'

'Oh shut up, Frank,' I said. But I was beaming like a loony from ear to ear.

'Well, Honey,' I said later, once the guests had gone and the mess had been cleared up and Mum had fallen asleep on the sofa with a party hat still on her head. 'I don't know about you, girl, but I certainly think this party has got to go down in pooch history, let alone any human-type version of history, as one to remember for ever and ever.' I stroked my adorable pupsicle and gave her a tickle under her chin.

And Honey put her head to one side in that gorgeous way she has and looked me straight in the eye as if to say, 'You can say that again!'

Can we do it all again next year?

Recipes

Try one of these easy dog food recipes and watch your pup smile.

Doggie Hamburger

> 250g minced meat, stir-fried in
>> 1 tbsp vegetable oil
>
> 2 boiled eggs, chopped
>
> 150g cooked plain oatmeal
>
> 125g puréed green beans
>
> 125g puréed carrots
>
> 2 tbsp cottage cheese

Instructions Combine all ingredients and shape into 'hamburgers'. Serve at room temperature.

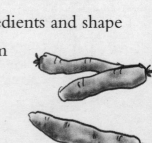

Doggie Casserole

250g boiled chicken, chopped

12g cooked brown rice

125g boiled mixed
 vegetables

3 to 4 tbsp unsalted chicken stock

Instructions Stir together and serve at room
temperature.

Peanut Butter Pooch Cookies* (see page 250)

600g whole wheat flour

60g white flour

60g oatmeal

1¼ tbsp baking powder

1 tbsp honey

250g peanut butter

250ml milk

249

Puppy Party

Instructions Combine flour, oatmeal and baking powder. Combine milk, peanut butter and honey in a separate bowl and mix well. Stir peanut butter mixture into flour/oatmeal mixture. Knead dough and roll out on floured surface to one centimetre thickness. Cut out treats using a cookie cutter. Place on aluminium foil on a baking sheet and bake in a 200 degree oven (gas mark 6) for approximately 15 minutes.

YUM!

* Be sure your dog has no wheat intolerance or nut allergy before cooking these, and if *you* are allergic to nuts, ask an adult to help you with this recipe.